DEAD OR ALIVE

DEAD OR ALIVE

PUTIN ON THE RITZ!

BOOK 3 OF THE MEL DREAD SERIES

John Kaufman

Dead or Alive Putin on the Ritz!

Printed in the United States of America
ISBN 978-1-64133-800-4 (sc)
ISBN 978-1-64133-801-1 (ebk)

2024.03.13

This book is printed on acid-free paper.

BlueInk Media Solutions
1111B S Governors Ave
STE 7582 Dover,
DE 19904

www.blueinkmediasolutions.com

Contents

Dedication

This book is dedicated to ending war in our troubled world. Let us all enjoy Peace on earth! God bless the Ukrainian people who continue dying in a fight against Russia's dictator, Vladimir Putin. Who is one of the many evil villains in my latest book, "Dead or Alive—Putin On The Ritz!"

Foreword

This one of a kind story is the third in the Melvin Dread action-packed series. In this high-flying sequel, Mel Dread and his partner Bonnie Starr are locked up in a Russian prison, serving life sentences.

The two Americans would be the first to ever escape alive from the prison's relentless, cold, dark—cruel history.

Quicker than a deathly head-on collision, Vladimir Putin, the Russian dictator, demands he wants the two American escape artists, dead or alive.

That's when this tall tale has deadly ins and outs, ups and downs. Some will live, and as in any good farce, some will have to die.

There is nothing Better Than a good mystery!

The author has written an action-packed spoof, a brilliantly written fast moving farce.

A farce is defined as comic dramatic work using buffoonery and horseplay. It typically includes crude characterization and ludicrously absurd, improbable situations, a story intended to make people laugh.

I've had fun creating another tall tale story, dedicated to all those who love reading my many books.

Behind Enemy Lines or Captivity Sucks!

S omewhere in a run-down prison, far away from his Ainsworth, Nebraska home, we find Mel Porter Dread III. After many failed attempts, he has finally succeeded in removing the chains and shackles that had been cutting into his ankles for days.

Mel was an expert at opening most locks. Still, like everything in this outdated, run-down Soviet prison, the rust and corrosion had slowly disrupted any feeling of a clean, cozy, place to live and die.

Mel was waiting for his daily meal of watered-down broth with a small loaf of bread. His water jug was empty. He, like many days, felt dehydrated.

Being in Russian captivity for the last eighteen months, he had endured cold, brutal conditions. While holding onto his belief that his friend Bonnie was alive and being held captive somewhere in this cruel, damp, dark labyrinth of human suffering.

One's survival skills often pivot around having keen ears and constantly listening. Mel could hear two prison workers getting the day's Food and water to all the cells. Especially those poor souls shackled to the wall. The noise from the outdated, rusted metal cart being pushed down the dark corridors sounded like the devil coming himself.

The cart screeching like finger nails on a blackboard once again came to a stop, and the two zombie-like men filled Mel's water jug and handed him his loaf of daily bread. While he waited for his ration of one ladle full of the same-looking stuff he had eaten every day since he arrived, which seemed like forever and a day.

"Hello do you speak English?" Mel would always ask the men pushing the cart in hopes of some communication.

The Two men dressed in dirty prison uniforms made some un-instinctive grunts, tongue tied slurred mumblings, finished their task, and moved on. As the sound of the rusty old cart was being pushed away, disappearing into the dank, musty-smelling darkness.

Von Trap Family Who or Somewhere High On A Hill Top!

S tupid was not a position for Someone as smart as Mel to find themselves incarcerated, cornered in a small foolish maze with no exits. Mel was confident that when he had figured out a plan, he would go to work to free himself. To locate his partner, Bonnie, to succeed escaping from their current incarceration predicament. The two friends, were captured locked up serving a life sentence in a Soviet prison.

With faith, God's help, Mel's Dreadful determination, along with lots of unbelievable luck, this would one day be a story he would no doubt tell his grandchildren. He would have lots of jaw-dropping tales and fascinating stories, that he hoped to live to share. How he and their mother, Bonnie, escaped the death grips of a hate-filled, twisted, tormented dark place made from the hideously barbaric madness of the Soviet Union's creation.

Hardly a day would pass that other inmates in the cell block would hear Mel singing in his cell, warming the damp, cold prison air with his love for music.

"There's no business like show business, like no business I know, everything about is exciting, everything about is a thrill, it's such a thrill! It's such a thrill, that's why everything's coming up roses for me and my gal." "We're getting married in the morning, Ding-dong, the bells are going to chime, la la la la, New York, New York! He was singing when he came to the conclusion that there was no better time than the present time to make some changes. Mel had been working on different escape scenarios. Having spent countless hours thinking that it was time for Someone other than the

Russians, to make the necessary changes in this down-and-out cesspool scenario. Where the damned would try to stay alive, living to survive, to cheat the death sentences they had been given.

With each passing day that, the dead, and those near death, would keep the prison crematory a warm place to be assigned to work in this seemingly endless cold Siberian landscape. There was seldom a time when new prisoners didn't arrive weekly on the Siberian railway to keep the prison full and the crematories burning endlessly.

"This, my dear Lord, is my prayer of love and thankfulness for another day to be blessed enough for this, my daily bread." "Amen!" Once again, as in past months, Mel carefully tore apart his loaf of bread, hoping once again to find something hidden inside. This day, he was surprised to see what appeared to be two hard-boiled eggs mysteriously tucked inside his somewhat hallow sounding loaf of bread. Many times to Mel's delight, Mel had often found hidden in his loaves' of bread. Finding inside, small hacksaw blades, chocolates, boiled potatoes, along with immense joy. Once, to his surprise, he discovered a Swiss pocket knife. Two weeks ago, he found a charm of a small heart that he had given Bonnie, removed from the beloved ankle bracelet she always wore.

Carefully trying to open the eggshell he soon realized the shells were hollow, except for the origami-folded paper he slowly pulled out from inside. He could see it was a Cootie Catcher, one of many designs Bonnie adored making and giving to others.

Holding the unfolded paper art up towards a sliver of light shining through a vent hole, allowed Mel to read what had been written on the folded paper. It was a square napkin with a drawing of a simple detailed map, along with a simple plan. It might be clear to Bonnie but not so much to him. That plan would include a key stuck inside tomorrow's bread. He thought having a key was a great place to start, but any successful escape plan would take action, courage and faith. Win or lose, the two kids from Nebraska, always praying for God's favor, were in a game of "Life or death," he would not quit now, with or without the key he had in his hand.

Deep in heavy thought, Mel mindlessly gazed at his loaf of bread, trying to paint a picture in his mentally decapitated brain how he and Bonnie would accomplish this impossible, never been-done Houdini escape trick. Every prison break attempt throughout its brutal history, had always ended in death. All the unfortunate souls who had bravely attempted to escape this deathly dark place, all died in vain.

The other prison cells that were in range of the Mel's entertaining sounds, were joyously listening. Some prisoners were actually learning to yodel along. The prison cell came alive when Mel would sing that popular song from the movie, "The Sounds of Music," sang by Julie Andrews, {Maria}, along with the Von Trap Family, singing the lyrics from "The Lonely Goatherd!"

Mel would announce to anyone wanting to sing, hum, or simply tap with a metal spoon on the bars, it would always start with Mel yelling "Heyo!" The sound resonating through the cold dark prison was met with the returning mixed echo's of those returning the sound of "Heyo!"

Followed by Mel bellowing out one of the prisoners favorite sing along songs.

"High on a hill was a lonely goatherd
Lay ee odl, lay ee odl, lay hee hoo
Loud was the voice of the lonely goatherd
Lay ee odl, lay ee odl-oo"
Folks in a town that was quite remote heard
Lay ee odl, lay ee odl, lay hee hoo
Lusty and clear from the goatherd's throat heard
Lay ee odl, lay ee odl-oo
(Umm)
Odl lay ee
(Odl lay ee)
Odl lay hee hee
(Odl lay hee hee)
Odl lay ee
Lay ee odl lay ee odl lay
Lay ee odl lay ee odl lay
Lay ee odl lay ee odl lay
Odl lay ee, old lay ee
Odl lay hee hee, odl lay ee
Odl lay odl lay, odl lay odl lee, odl lay odl lee
Odl lay odl, lay odl lay
Hoo

May I Have This Dance or A Doomed Dread Person!

"It was later that day, "Yes, of course," Talking to himself, "I am aware of the ice-cold Siberian tundra and the inhospitable weather conditions outside the prison. I'm not stupid," dancing like Mike Tyson, making quick, sharp japs at his make-believe opponents. "La la la... I could have danced all night. I could have danced all night," {musical pause.} They would have no choice but to escape unnoticed, navigating through the checkpoints to the main gate with every step choreographed flawlessly. Their only chance at freedom would be to vanish, to become somehow invisible. Getting to and boarding the passenger train without phony or otherwise documents was concerning and unlikely. An alternative was whether they could jump-hitch a ride if that's what they had to do—like hobos and those cross-country stow-aways—well hidden in one of the many cargo cars on this sprawling railway, with its countless stops heading west, with its final destination, Mosco.

Mel wanted to believe they could escape the hell of this place, exchanging it for freedom. Mel made a cross on his chest and raised his head, eyes wide open. He stared into the darkness. "Please hear my cry, oh dear lord. Without your help, your blessings, I am most surely a doomed man. Knowing in my heart when it is my time to go, I will die with a soul born of your inherent greatness, living and dying by my savior God's intentions. Protect and watch over me until all my earthly duties are done, and death brings me back to be with you. Amen!"

One thing was sure: Mel did not intend to go anywhere without his beloved partner, his best friend, Bonnie.

Their odds were zero percent of pulling this escape off was just what it was, merely impossible. Many incarcerated souls through the prison's long history ended up dead trying. No man or woman ever escaped this place of hell on earth. All those poor souls that through the years were locked away with little hope of surviving very long in such deplorable conditions. Nothing much had changed including the yearly number of prison deaths, due to illness, drugs, suicide, aids, along with those who fit the category of cause of death, unknown! Which meant the prisons disposal system was in good working order.

The prison facts meant nothing to the kid-duo, currently a duo-less kid. He would start by finding his soulmate. Together, they had the brains and the talent to beat any odds. As of now, Mel had yet to learn how he would do it. But not knowing had never stopped him in the past, and it would not stop him now.

Dipping a chunk of bread into his slop bowl, he was happy, excited, and more hopeful than he had felt in a long time. It would be another of those cold nostalgic lonely evenings when Mel wrapped himself then would quietly sing to himself songs from all his grampa's old collection of 45 RPM records he loved to listened to, he would end his day with "All I Have To Do Is Dream!" by the Everly Brothers."

"Drea-ea-ea-ea-eam, dream, dream, dream
Drea-ea-ea-ea-eam, dream, dream, dream
When I want you in my arms
When I want you and all your charms
Whenever I want you, all I have to do is
Drea-ea-ea-ea-eam, dream, dream, dream"
"When I feel blue in the night
And I need you to hold me tight
Whenever I want you,
all I have to do is Drea-ea-ea-ea-eam
I can make you mine,
taste your lips of wine
Anytime night or day
Only trouble is, gee whiz

I'm dreamin' my life away"
"I need you so that I could die
I love you so and that is why
Whenever I want you,
all I have to do is
Drea-ea-ea-ea-eam, dream, dream, dream Drea-ea-ea-ea-eam"
"I can make you mine,
taste your lips of wine
Anytime night or day
Only trouble is, gee whiz
I'm dreamin' my life away
I need you so that I could die
I love you so and that is why
Whenever I want you,
all I have to do is
Drea-ea-ea-ea-eam, dream, dream, dream
Drea-ea"

Stop Loafing Around or Tasty Toasted Iron—Enriched!

From the beginning, the mysterious person loading Mel's loaves of bread had the intense smell and taste of his dear friend, Bonnie, whom he had missed every day since they were separated.

It was a blessing to know the truth. No more wondering day in and day out if the other was dead or alive. Now he knew they both were being held in this same prison and very much both not dead, but alive!

Bonnie had become quite the favorite prisoner, having been promoted to the most wanted job in prison, working in the kitchen. The Food was never that good any way you prepared it, but those in the kitchen never went hungry. Nor had it seemed as if anyone had connected Bonnie's association to Mel. Who now knew the person working in the kitchen baking his bread was his one and only dear friend, Bonnie. Who would soon let it be known she was not only innovative in the kitchen. She was one tough female with an I.Q. of 140, was crazy-time-smart, and was fully aware that everyone wants to Rule the World, "laughing, 'me included." Singing to herself "Everybody wants to rule the world," she could not remember any other words to the song, so she just kept repeating that one line she knew. "Everybody wants to rule the world…"

It was another early cold Tuesday morning when the prison delivery trucks were in wait for the Siberian Railway Trains' arrival. The prison workers would be ready to unload the prison's cargo of food and supplies, which the prison received every third Tuesday of the month.

Back at the prison, Bonnie with the other kitchen workers were busy making and baking loaves of bread. One loaf, in particular, would soon reach Mel's padlocked prison cell, where a key would soon be in his tight-fisted grasp. With no idea as to what the key went to or what it could unlock. He had high hopes it was some master key that could be used to their advantage.

Moronic Russians or Snap-Crackle-Pop!

Like everywhere, drugs in a Russian Prison were bartering tools for negotiations between prisoners and prison employees, guards, and policing staff. A few powerful thugs ran the place with a cutthroat Maffia mentality. The two kids from Nebraska had been well acquainted with the moronic Russians years earlier when Bonnie had set fire that burned the Russian's secret enemy's compound and headquarters, long ago in the faraway country called America. Unfortunately, it would be the reason they both had been put on a Russian bounty hunters list. Mel, and Bonnie had thought that by changing their identity, they could fade into the woodwork. Left with the foggy memories, of mostly two forgotten young kids, leaving no rhyme or reason to where they had disappeared, or their whereabouts.

The two had been followed unknowingly by the well trained Soviet professional bounty hunters. Who had without much effort located, Melvin and Bonnie's unknown where abouts. where they had been chloroformed, drugged, and smuggled out of the country back to Russia. The two were sentenced to life in a Siberian prison without a trial. The two young American prisoners became known only as Inmate #97530 and Inmate #97540.

Mel could only hope and wait, wait and hope. Thinking like a skilled detective, Mel had already been putting together his escape plan. Unfortunately, all he had was a key from his last loaf of bread. Leaving him to impatiently continue waiting for a signal from prisoner #97530 that she had a plan. Because prisoner #97540 was clueless.

It was again late afternoon as Mel waited for his one meal of the day. Hearing the hideous sounds of the old metal food cart was the same routine as every meal before. Holding out his dry water jug, he waited his turn. He wondered if he used his key now, all might be forfeited in a botched effort to gain the upper hand in a world devoted to torturing inmates. Faster than a Russian split second he and his cohort would, if caught, be put to death.

Putting his water jug down, then grasping tightly to his bowl, today's soup, for once, smelled good. He took it and set it carefully down. With outstretched arms, he reached for the loaf of bread. Showing his appreciation, he kindly thanked them with a simple "God Bless you both." In a queer yet familiar voice, one of the two men who had just handed Mel his loaf of bread replied, "You do the same, Mr. Melvin Porter Dread III, same time tomorrow. As always, I'll see you in my dreams."

Faster than a flash of lightning striking the ground, snap, crackle, and pop! It was over. Mel's mind felt like a confused deer caught in a speeding car's headlights. Stunned, his mind was scrambling to catch up. He was brought back to reality by the unnerving sound of the metal cart being quickly pushed away into the darkened obese. He was clutching his loaf of bread to his chest. "Oh my Lord in heaven," as tears of surprise and happiness rolled down Mel's face. It was like butter sweet icing on his cake! Like raindrops falling from the sky. "Raindrops keep falling, dada da. Yahoo praises God from whom all blessings flow." He extending his arms toward the heavens, hands grasping his daily bread, he thanked and praised his God almighty, ending with a heartfelt joyous Amen."

Like a master in clinical dissection, he carefully tore the bread into little pieces and ate it with his soup. Tonight's soup must have been stolen from the food made for the paid Russian staffers, and those higher elite people holding positions in this maximum-security prison. It had taken him some time to finish his soup. At about the same time, he had run out of bread. Noticing something on his cell floor that appeared to be the size of an extra-long hot dog, wrapped in tin foil that someone must have slipped into his cell. Cautiously, he opened the small bundle and carefully looked at the documents issued to Aleksei Anastasiy, personnel Secretary, Secret Administrator. Aka. Undercover S.P.I.N.A.C.H division.

Well, Mel thought, my detective friend must be hanging around with some pretty unique people and high-up places. There must be secret rooms, unknown location, where Bonnie must be waitering or catering to the prison employees playing poker with other top prison officials.

He tried not to think about who she did to whom, for what would always be water under the bridge? Life is not kind or compassionate, especially when trying to stay alive as a vulnerable female inmate in a Russian prison housing primarily "take what they want," horny men. With all his love and devotion, Mel knew his trust and faith would give him the strength to overcome any pain in his mind, heart, and soul. He spent the next few hours trying to pronounce his new name. Alekei Anatastasiy. Mi name Alekei Anatastasiy; he had long ago captured the accent of his Russian enemies. Finally, Mel drifted off to sleep. His frequent crazy dreams had become a part of his nightly head games—that game of the conscious versus the unconscious, a contact sport played all out in his one-of-a-kind, mysterious brain.

It was Tuesday, which meant the train with all its cargo, Food, supplies, and miscellaneous items, including newly convicted prisoners had once again arrived. In the bakery, Bonnie had a new name tag on her kitchen uniform pinned to her shirt, "MaRiya, Mariya BapBapa Varvara."

Two guardsmen unlocked the big iron doors to the loading dock, and two other corrections officers watched as big trucks were pulled in, and the security gate quickly locked again. The smell of fresh baking bread permeated the air, making the kitchen seem like the best place to be if you are held captive and sentenced to life in the Russian prison system.

In two days, the cargo from Tuesday's delivery will have been unloaded, and the outgoing garbage, waste products, and the outgoing personnel, workers, convicts, and others holding transfer papers, could board the train, traveling back west, towards Mosco by railway.

In the next few hours, Bonnie's escape plans would be what Mel would find inside his Tuesdays and Wednesdays Sourdough Bread.

Mel was in deep fear that if caught, Mariya along with her friend Aleksei Anastasiy, would be put to death by hanging, or shot in the back running for their freedom.

Trying to empower his positive consciousness. "It ain't gonna happen," calmly reassuring himself his fate was never destined to be shot or hung to death in this stinking Russian Hell Hole.

It had been another restless night for Mel. Not having slept much Tuesday night, tonight would soon turn into Thursday. Mel could only wait for the secret sign or signs that the planned escape was underway. Mel sat on the edge of his hard paddling-less mattress, hearing the old rusty food cart being pushed his way. The food cart was early, and that had only happened a few times in the past. Mel could only wait as the noisy cart stopped, then in a low voice came, "Are you ready?" As a key was put into the lock and turned. The cell door creaked as it was pushed open. Quickly handing Mel a quick change of prison worker men's clothes that he slipped into. There was no speaking as he mimicked his friend and began helping her move the rusty cart back toward the kitchen compound.

Once back inside the kitchen, the metal doors that separated the kitchen from the prisoner sections were closed and locked with security people and staffers, and workers could feel safer.

"Do you have the key I gave you detective?"

Shaking his head, Yes! "I have it tied to my Junk. You know, my family jewels!"

"Great hiding place. "No one would ever think to find what you had in your prison trousers," pushing him into the walk-in freezer."

"What the," Somewhat confused, resisting, trying hard to stand his ground. "You're shoving me into cold storage, what for?"

"For now Melvin Porter Dread, just do what I say. You have the key to open the door from the inside, which remains locked without a key. I have a big party to attend. Fortunately, I will be one of the few fortunate prisoners to oversee those invited to this very special one day that the prison celebrates, January 7, Christmas day in the Soviet Union. "The entire prison by this time tomorrow afternoon will find out what it feels like when you mess round with Missy Pissy Me."

The small select kitchen staff had assembled a feast for this one short day. It was one day when good old Russian Vodka was plentiful. How and what people consumed this festive drunken night would haunt minds for a long time to come. The two kids from Ainsworth, Nebraska, had once again started living up to their reputation as two super hero's who once again were in the process of kicking the Russian hemorrhoidal asses.

Mel had nearly stopped shaking from the cold freezer air. The "inside thermostat" was beginning to look like the temperature was on the rise. He was not destined to freeze to death, thinking; "Thank God From Whom All Blessings Come!"

Meanwhile, the men and twenty or so females were getting intoxicated at this one-day of the year Christmas celebration. All participating in singing Russian Christmas folksongs. This year the overly-sung song would be "JOY TO THE WORLD," which means Joy only for Russian born citizens.

Радуйся, мир!

Радуйся, мир, Христос рождён! Прими Царя царей; Радуйся, мир! Христос пришел. В церквях поют о Нем. Поля, сады, леса, холмы Им вторят с торжеством

Им вторят, вторят с торжеством. Чтоб в сердце твоем приют Он нашел

ewᵛᵉ Translation

Joy to the World, the Lord is come! Let earth receive her King; Let every heart prepare Him room, And Heaven and nature sing, And Heaven and nature sing, And Heaven, and Heaven, and nature sing.

It would seem that some of these partiers, those who should have been paying attention to Bonnies behind scenes activities were going unnoticed. With God's blessing, and a lot of good old Russian vodka, a banquet table covered with an array of fancy assorted foods, filled with lots of mind altering contra-ban that Bonnie had found in a storage room, that was posted a big red warning sign, Poison-Danger-Poison-Danger. Restricted Area! Stay Out!

Like well-greased wagon wheels, the night was rolling forward as planned. Bonnie posing as Mariya is about to lead her first wardrobe change away from the view of others. She quietly begins by leading a drunken prison guard back to the walk-in freezer. Seductively, with deadly lover's passion, she wrapped her leg around his leg. When she leaned over pretending to give the guy a French kiss, in one quick move pushed a couple of pills in the guy's unsuspecting drunken gullet. To assure he swallowed the pills, she plowed her tongue down his throat, having had her way with what was not a bad looking Russian. Flipping off the interior lighting, she opened the freezer door, without much trouble; and like the local pizza parlor, delivered her hand-tossed random person who without any struggle, surrendered what he had been wearing, to Mel. Like a quick-change-artist, he was now newly outfitted, and ready to disco dance his way out the prisons front gates. Dressed to kill in his "getting out of here" street clothes, smelling much like the party he had been enticed away from. Appearing to be impeccable, attired in size 44 m-l, he would be dressed to look the part of Alexsei Anastasiy, who would confidently walk out the front gate, get on a train, and escape on this blessed January 7th Soviet Christmas Eve.

At this particular time, those partygoers attending last night's party would be primarily incapacitated or passed out due to a lot of drinking, along with a heavy slurry of comatose prison drugs. That were no longer stored in a locked room. They would eventually show up as gone, gone missing. They were not missing, just purposely misplaced. The drinks and food all intensely saturated with plenty of alcohol, along with a shit load of mind-altering drugs. Just ask anyone who attended the Miriya Crystal Meth Christmas celebration. This year's caterer would be remembered for years to come. Prisoner #97530 had far outdone the festivities of past year's parties, making this celebration most rememberable of all.

It was a party that had quickly became comatose, and before the night was officially over, the two Nebraska kids had packed two medium suitcases that Bonnie had earlier hidden in the walk-in-freezer. Mel was not surprised to find Bonnie had left him a water-filled wash bowl, soap, cologne, a razor, and the softest towel smelling of the girl he had been in love with since the beginning of time: his hero, his soul mate, his partner in this life, Mariya, formerly referred to as prisoner #97530.

Home is Where You Can Find it or Little Dread People!

L iving in busy, overcrowded Los Angeles, California, had lost its appeal to Mel's mother and father; shortly after, Mel and his friend Bonnie disappeared. Now, almost two years later, most people assumed they were more than likely dead. Mel's dad was declared the sole beneficiary of the old family farm. If Mel and Bonnie were dead, with or without a corpse, the secret to the Dread family fortune of gold coins would remain unknown. Once again becoming a continuation of the two hundred year hunt for the remaining gold coins that had been found were once again a hidden mystery.

Until the coin's location had been rediscovered, it would be a new twist into the on-again, off-again decades-old, ongoing family mystery. Mel's dad, a retired minister, had, more or less, lost his unrelenting faith in religious ideology. Mel's mom was recovering from a long illness that had left her having to use a wheelchair. Being a very successful business tycoon, she had been scathed, true, but her money was a blessing. Her money was used to rebuild the old Dread family farm using Mel's architectural drawings they had found among his belongings. These drawings had become one of their many cherished keepsakes. Now they were over seeing their son's dreams being carried out in his memory. Since the house had been completed, it just sat there, as if waiting for some happy somebodies to move in and live happily forever. Everyone in the community hoping and praying every day, it would be those two young people, Mel with his partner Bonnie beside him, would return to live in the empty house.

Keeping faith that somehow, someday, the two missing kids would come home, and move back to the cherished, very much loved, Dread family homestead. Which included them someday having a number of healthy, happy, thriving little Dread people.

Escapades In The Freezer or
Like Flies On Sticky Paper!

I t was nearing the midnight hour. The train would begin loading the outgoing passengers traveling on tonight's train, heading to its returning destination of Mosco. Where it would turn around once again, traveling back on the same tracks, three hundred and sixty-five days of the year, minus the hours the train spent broken down, needing repairs or hung-up somewhere due to bad weather or track problems. It, like all things Russian, had the smell of old stale Vodka. Such a big country was quickly running out of soldiers, using the country's prison population to fight in Russia's ongoing war with Ukrane. Vladimir Putin's total lack of consciousness, his inhuman carelessness regard for anyone's life but his own. Refusing to give-up his insane on going unenlightened, soulless aggression.

Hiding in the walk-in freezer, taking a loving moment arms around one another, the two young superheroes kissed one final time. It was now or never! Slowly, they pushed the big freezer door open, quickly taking a peek out, grabbing Mel's jacket sleeve, giving it a little tug, everything was a go.

The two American impersonators were skilled in the craft of showing up with people's persona's, so far, so good, as they moved towards the exit signs, trying to look as if they were not out of place. Several corrections officers paid little notice to the two as they passed the men. They were prepared and had in their hands their official visitor passes. Stopping at the final gate, they handed the man their credentials. The guy looked into their face's, took a quick look at their papers, then after a few tense moments, the automatic doors were opened, then quickly closed behind them. They continued toward the train station a few blocks away.

The cold night air seemed to fill the train station causing the chattering of teeth, as they advances in a single line. One at a time, handing the ticket person their papers. He nodded at the two travelers, "Hello," and both nodded back in return. As the train's whistle echoed the train's departure, he quickly stamped their boarding passes as they jumped aboard. The Door slammed shut behind them as another rail steward greeted them, looked at each of their train passes, and motioned them to follow him. He led them to their sleeper bunkers. They were in car number ten, bunker Twelve. They hoped this would be home for the next few days. Their sleeper car was three cars forward from the dining car, right next to the bar. Following closely behind somewhere at the end of the train they both assumed was a Kabuse.

Most of the travelers were already in their births sleeping, as it was late, and soon they would fall asleep next to each other. The extra-ordinary young couple who would eventually become known as the two people in the prison's history to have master-minded a diabolical prison escape. Just two skinny kids from a small mid-west town, having escaped, successfully traveling aboard, Russia's Trans Siberian Railroad. The longest rail line in the world, 5,771 Miles {9,288 km} Mosco to Vladivostok a port city near the Chinese Korean borders.

It was early morning at the prison. Not many had recovered from a hard night of partying. At the end of the evening, a small lake of cheap Russian Vodka had been consumed. However, if the truth is told, there were also enough illicit drugs in the food prepared. The food, the drink everyone had eaten' and consumed was turning the Russian's into dumb-ass baboon's. She had made monkeys out of them all. She had them right where prisoner #97530 planned. Carried out flawlessly, even the un-spiked punch tasting of a subtle hint of mint flavoring had been heavily laced with psychedelic drugs. It was when prisoner #97530 in charge of the bakery could not be found or located that it now was becoming a sudden big concern. It was clear with the lacking smell of freshly baking bread could only mean one thing. Without anyone in the bakery overseeing the making of the dough, the prisoner's daily loaf of hard-crusted wheat bread would not be on today's rusty old food cart. Therefore, there would no bread on this day, just drinking water, and a large ladle of a thick slurry the prisoners called "gloopy-doa-slope." In English, it translated to roughly meaning "the soup made from the stuff that hungry and starving dogs refused to eat!

When you are incarcerated behind bars in a Siberian Soviet Prison, it is designed to guarantee you won't like it—especially those prisoners who were in solitary confinement or, worse, assigned to hard labor, which was, in all reality, a death sentence.

The now incognito duo, posing as industrial manufacturing salespeople, were gingerly returning from the baggage car. It was a treasure trove, a banquet all for their taking, stuff the two would use to get past suspicious yet hopefully unsuspecting Russian checkpoints. So much locked baggage in one box car, all ready for Mel to easily pick open the locks, quickly going through others belongings, taking anything they might be able to use, abiding by that old adage "All is fair in love and war."

Two new travelers with newly acquired identification would show they were a handicapped couple, suffering from many ailments, including being deft and nearly blind. Their papers stated they were traveling west for eye surgery at a Mosco Eye Clinic.

The timing was everything regarding theater, comedy, and knowing when you should not be seen on center stage. So far, there had been a couple of designated short stops, short layovers along the train's long route. Passengers got off the train while others waited to board. Deciding it was a good time to now change their identities to begin posing as the couple traveling blind, mute, man and woman. Last seen being escorted off the train by what looked to be a couple of nurses. The blind travelers never got back on the train, suspiciously curious.

The Trains horn bellowed loudly, piercing the cold night air, now moving once again heading toward their next destination. Meanwhile, back at the train station, those two mutes, blind people had somehow been locked in a janitor's room until many hours later, their kicking on the door would be finally heard, and would finally be discovered.

There came a lot of questions from the train authorities that no one could answer. Who, what, why, and did this have anything to do with the two escaped prisoners who were still on the lamb, still not apprehended? The Russian officials would be taking swift action. Soviet soldiers, heavily armed, were in place, waiting to board the train at its next stop in the town of Celjabinsk. Their mission would be to storm the train, catching the passengers on board off guard, thoroughly searching each car, from front to rear, top to bottom systematical. In hopes of taking into their custody the two escaped American prisoner #97530, and her counter part prisoner #97540.

Knock knock who's there, it was Mel having one of his hunches, "Bonnie, or whatever I'm now supposed to be calling you," holding a newspaper blocking their faces, pretending to read. "We are in mortal danger!"

Peeking out from the side of the newspaper, quickly checking to see that they weren't being watched. "Mortal danger, Mr. Blind, deft and dumb, should we find a place to hide?"

"Us finding an optimal place to hide just might save our lives." She squeezed his hand and whispered, " I am stuck on you like a fly on the sticky paper right behind you, Mel." Making their way to the train car they found earlier to be a possible great hiding spot, a place out of the sight of others. It was in two cars that all contained items that were crated in large wooden boxes of all sizes. On each box was the information of content, its weight, where it was from, and the destinated city's where the train made regular stops to load and unload People and their stuff.

They knew that the whistle from the train was the signal they would soon be at the next stop.

Boxed Ready To Go or Your A Circus-Clown-Try To Fit In!

"It is totally dark here, Mel; how can you see?"

"I can't," taking her hand, the two of them managing to crawl through the maze of boxes.

Reaching into his bag, Mel pulled out a pocket flashlight.

"Well, you never cease to amaze me, Mr. whoever you are pretending to be now." Taking a deep breath, "is this where you have chosen for us to hide?"

"Yes," pointing the light at the side of the box." Both reading: "Putin Entertainment!" Slowing down, with the train still moving, was boarded by a bunch of clowns dressed as Russian military police. Systematically searching for the two escapee's that are believed to be aboard this train. With Putin's instructions to shoot to kill! Then lie like a Russian leader explained with a fabricated bunch of made up stories.

They had little time to spare as Mel lifted open the big hinged wooden crate lid. "Let me help you get in Missy," helping to push her butt into the grate. He jumped up, threw his six-pack somewhat scrawny abs across the edge of the crate, like a professional dumpster diver, went in head first, scooting in next to his sidekick, together they lowered the lid of the large circus container.

Bonnie holding the flashlight while Mel, as fast as he could, ingeniously wired the box's lid from the inside so it could not be opened without having to pry it open from the outside.

"You're so smart," hugging him and asking, "Speaking of death, I might die of starvation," reaching for Mel's bag, "I know there is stuff for us to eat in your bag, or my name is not Agathie Christy."

"You don't even know who Agathie Christy is?"

"She is my favorite author who I read occasionally, but only after I have something to take my mind off my grumbling stomach noise's." Reaching for the bag, they both froze— as they could hear men entering the box car. The men began systematically searching the areas around the cargo containers, one soldier mulled around the crate they were hiding inside of, but didn't sound as if they were opening any crates or oversized boxes.

You could hear the men moving about. Bonnie and Mel were as quiet as black mold growing in a moist butt crack. They both knew from past experiences there were lots of worst places to be, as they soon realized that this was a great hiding place—a crate packed with circus clown costumes, including all the accessories, and a ton of clown face make-up. After extensive search of the entire train, the disappointed soldiers gave the all clear signal to the train engineer, who sounded the trains whistle two times letting it be known the Siberian Railway was up and running once more. The two stow aways were much more relaxed after they were not found by the men who had searched the train.

Bonnie, speaking of clowns! Do you remember the words to "Send In The Clown's!?"

"Well if I can't remember the song you and I practiced for months, expecting to perform in a lamb-brained local talent show that never happened because we were the only talented people signed up to participate. You start singing I'll join in like we not that long ago practiced singing one of the most recorded songs. I'll hum, you join in, and I will follow your lead." Hmmmmmmmmmmmm... "Isn't it rich?

Are we a pair?
Me here at last on the ground
You in mid-air
Where are the clowns?"
"Isn't it bliss?
Don't you approve?
One who keeps tearing around

One who can't move
Where are the clowns?
Bonnie joining in.
"Just when I'd stopped opening doors
Finally knowing the one that I wanted was yours
Making my entrance again with my usual flair
Sure of my lines
No one is there."
"Don't you love farce?
My fault, I fear
I thought that you'd want
what I want
Sorry, my dear"
Mel, "But where are the clowns?
Send in the clowns"
Don't bother, they're here."
Bonnie, "Isn't it rich?
Isn't it queer
Losing my timing this late
In my career?"
Beautiful singing together,
"But where are the clowns?"
"I don't see the Clowns"
"There ought to be clowns"
"Well, maybe next year..."

Where's The Beef? Or This Is A Nifty Hiding Place!

They both could hear what sounded like the car's sliding outer doors opening.

They both sat frozen as they could hear the commotion of men outside their crate—the big oversized toy box painted with circus elephants and colorful clowns began to levitate. Then, a forklift carefully removed the crate from the train, labeled: ***"Putin's Traveling Circus Extravaganza and Sideshow."*** The two brainiac kids dressed ready to go to work, the currently out of work clowns from Ainsworth Nebraska hiding unsuspiciously inside. Whether they liked it or not, Mel and Bonnie would unofficially become part of the many other clowns performing in tonight's "Putin's Big Top and Side Show Circus." It was grand opening tonight, in front of a sold out crowd. In tonight's audience would be several prestigious people. The man who seemed to be running the show was a man who looked very much like Putin himself. Could it be true the leader of the Soviet Union Vladimir Putin would make a rare appearance during this big grand opening night?

Nothing it seems is much better to a cold-hearted Russian than spending time in early spring when the Circus comes to town. Comes to pitch their big top tents in the old city of Orsk, Russia, with a population of 222,298, give or take a few thousand, depending on who you ask. Any time Putin's circus is in any town, whether residents want to or not, every citizen is expected to wear their Putin rubber mask. While showing their support for their leader the week the Soviet-run circus is in town. The circus posters had been posted on every prominent street corner. The posters subtle message commanding townspeople of Orsk to buy their tickets for the entire family early, to reserve their place in the grandstands before the sitting capacity for each night's performances of *"Putin on the Ritz" had been booked* and sold out.

It had been about three hours, and the two prison escapees had spent the time quietly talking and catching up. The flashlight illuminated the big wooden crate full of circus costumes, shoes, funny hats, and all the clown makeup. In the past, the two detectives have relied heavily on their ability to disguise themselves when needed. "Well, how do I look," Mel asked his assistant as she worked to get his orange and purple clown wig positioned. "Yes sir, Boss, you look like one scary-assed-circus clown."

"Well Missy, your get-up with the brillo pad bronze-colored hair, taking this moment to pat myself on my back, for my artistic talent, for your out of this world, sad-faced expression I painted on you. Handing her a big red nose. "Looking good Fraulein Ddjektiv! That means "Starr" in German."

"Danka shoone! Heir Dready or not. "I cannot wait to get out of this box to be the clown I've always hoped and wished I could one day be." Working to get her nose stuck to her clown-painted face.

"Ya Vo! Copy that."

Mel with his adrenaline searing, unfastened the wire securing the lid closed from the inside. Slowly lifting the crate's wooden top enough to rule out any potential dangers. The coast looked clear as they both climbed out of their nifty hideaway, "Now what," Bonnie inquired as she worked to keep her red nose to stay on. "This way, follow me and remember we are speech and deaf Russian commoners who found work by joining the Circus.

"Understood," Bonnie just smiled and shook her head that she was best when playing the clown who had no voice, just a hand held honk, honk, honking horn.

It's Only Elephant Poop or Putin On Your Best Face!

The next day would be another challenge to fool the other clowns who had noticed the two never seen before, these two new individuals working diligently to set up the big tent for tonight's opening show. Soon the atmosphere full of people, the smell of heavily buttered popcorn, looming there along with all the other enoculas mixed smelling aromas, like wet sand and elephant poop.

Every seat was occupied, it was a filled to capacity. The crowds fever pitched enthusiasm quieted as the house lighting was dimmed to complete darkness. In the darkened stark silence, a big spot light fixed and focused on the circus ring master holding a microphone loudly welcoming each and every person from near and far, here to be apart of, Putin's all-new "Big Top Exstavigani" premiere presentation.

"Witamy wszystkich i każdego z Was na premierowej prezentacji rosyjskiego „Putina Big Top Exstavigani".

Putin's on the Ritz celebration was under way. The long parade of elephants, Zebras, Monkeys, performing dogs, performers in tights, men swallowing fire, and those crazy-assed clowns would be forced down the big gun's barrel, then shot out of the over-sized canon, blasting the guy who dared to get in the gun barrel then shot through the air. A clown's head followed by the daring young man's body, all of him pointing towards an enormously small net, suspended in the air, on the opposite side of the enormous tent. As always, it would seem the clowns were what made a night that you would never forget. Yes sir boss! Putin's Big Top Circus had it all painted faces, endless mischievous silliness, laughing, popcorn, and cotton candy.

Yeah, Bonnie thought, "fun," as she ran behind the parading elephants with a big shovel scooping up paca-dermis-poop and trying not to get any sha-poo on her outfit. It was her job to scoop$_N$-toss, making sure to be carefully getting it into the crapcarts that the clowns were pushing around the parade of animals in the conga line.

The Big Top's three-hour show had been advertised as "The Best Circus in the Universe. As countless times before, tonight's festive opening would honor "*Mr. Vladimir Putin*," Russia's beloved clown himself. With a couple of Rubles, they were making a killing on the selling of latex Putin look-alike face masks of the man himself. There were alot of seats in the bleachers, and the place was filled beyond capacity with many people wearing their Putin mask.

With so many things going on at once, the concoction of sounds were over the top, filled with the grand master asking everyone to look right center stage, where a spotlight pointed at a giant cannon. Three muscular assistants, acting like "The Three Stooges" but built like Russian female athletes on a steady diet of muscle-building steroids, had the crowd's attention. They humorously fought and struggled to get a smaller clown inside the cannon's barrel. Everyone, including the circus parade, paused as the cannon fuse was lit. Mel the clown in the cannon was familiar with people being shot out of such devices; he held his breath as he heard the crowd chanting ten, nine, eight, seven, six, five, four, three, two, one. KABOOM.

10 - десятп (desjat') 9 - девятп (devjat') 8 - восемг (vosem') 7 - семп (sem') 6 - шестп) 5 - пятп (pjat') (šest') 4 - четыре (četyre3 - три (tri) 2 - два (dva) : 1 - один (odin) Бабах бум. Translation of «kaboom» бабах бум.

Russian To Get Out or Big Top Flip-Flop!

E veryone's eyes were frozen wide open. Everyone watching was mesmerized as the small clown who had, against his will, been forced into the cannon moments earlier, was no longer in the cannon.

Mel's arms in front of him resembled a capless Clark Kent dressed in a clown costume going faster than a speeding bullet. Screaming like a guy just shot out of a canon who had completely missed the intended target painted clearly on the apparent undersized net. Still in perpetual motion, he desperately tried to grab hold of anything he could to break his momentum. Putin's big grand opening night of fun and festivity would take a sudden wrong turn when Mel single-handedly was dangling from some supporting tent ropes, which might have been why the entire canvas tent was noticeably beginning to collapse. In terrifying fear, the audience started to move toward the exits. It was not a night anyone attending would soon forget, especially those injured during the mass exodus. Putin's face masks were still on children's heads as everyone quickly as they possibly could, were scrambling for their lives. Here a Putin, there a Putin, everywhere you looked there were look-a-like Vladimir Putin's. The Sea of look-a-like circus goers were all actively participating in the madness, being pulled, pushed, and shoved out of harm's way as the once oversized canvas tent had been reduced to resembling an enormous lumpy canvas pancake.

Hundreds of people were still trapped under the collapsing, heavy, dilapidating skin of the tent's dead weight. The canvas tent carcass was squirming as if it were full of hungry larvae. All those images of people struggling to escape, saturated in the toxic, ear-deafening sounds of chaotic madness.

Bonnie was way ahead of the cannon fuse being lit. She had handed her poop shovel to a Putin-wearing man sitting in the first row. In full mime, the crowd laughed as Bonnie, the clown, showed her replacement how to keep everyone laughing while scooping up poop. Gone, she disappeared heading out of sight, she hurried over to where the cannon had been pointed towards a suspended net, laser lights directing all eyes to a pulsating bullseye, continued strobing amongst the pile of the circus's dead remains. Looking like it had been completely covered with a canvas sheet, as if it was a burial shroud in respect for the dead.

The loud commotion left the two supposedly deaf and mute circus clowns choosing to depart A.S.A.P., but not before running through the food tent, where everyone there had hastily vacated. The scores of people running to help the terrible alarming sounds of countless helpless people screaming, along with those unmistakable snap-crackle-pop of the tents-supporting wooden poles breaking into maybe some usable firewood.

The two of them alone in the food tent was now a game of beat the clock. With no one to stop them, the strategy was to run as fast as possible, grabbing anything helpful to avoid spending another night in their makeup and clown outfit. It had been an excellent, successful ruse. As they like mash and grab thugs, grabbed bottled water, stuff to eat, warmer clothing, tools, weapons, and maybe be lucky enough to find some cash.

They both knew their way around the food tent pretty well. After all, the two clowns from Ainsworth had been scoping out the place while eating meals there since posing as newly hired circus employees. It was a quick and easy heist of the food tent. They had taken the Clown outfits off and were now dressed in everyday-looking clothing. Jeans, flannel outerwear, each toting a backpack filled with coveted treasures, the rewards of their exclusive five-finger tactical maneuvers discount. Both calmly exit the food tent proceeding to walk towards a distant parking lot, where they plan to borrow a ride to a safer place, like Nebraska—standing in the vast parking lot with rows of Russian cars with Russian plates.

"Come on, Mel, let's speed it up; find us a ride. It's not like we're here to buy the damn car!" Bonnie circled a row of parked cars, pulling feverishly on door handles, looking for one not overly endowed with door locks, steering wheel locking devices, and alarm sirens randomly being set off. The circus parking lot should have been the perfect place to hijack a ride out of there. They were not being picky! They would take anything with four wheels with good rubber, one with a few more good miles left in it. One that would get them to the highway where they could blend into the traffic already on the road. But they were having no luck. Mel knew they were running out of time, and people were starting to head toward the parking lot. The sound of police cars, medical ambulances, fire trucks, rescue crews, and people wandering around looking for their vehicles all added to the mass confusion.

Taking Bonnie's hand, their backpacks on their shoulders, Mel instinctively sensed immediate danger as, hand in hand, they marched toward the circus exit road leading to the highway. He had already rethought his old escape plan, which did not require putting any foot to the petal or rubber to the road.

Inflation On The Rise or American Circus Clowns Fly Free.

I n Russia, there is no such thing as a petty thief. There was no distinction between stealing a Doughnut or the vendor's doughnut cart. When caught, you become the viper's next meal. *"Just another dirty rat."* Taken off the food chain.

At the end of the road, seeing nothing, except of all things, just sitting there for them to climb aboard and steal a Russian hot air balloon that looked like Vladimir Putin's over inflated head. It was the head and clown painted face of the man himself, Vladimir Putin. There was no time to think. Bonnie did not need Mel to pull to get her in the Hot air balloon, advertising the Circus was in town. It looked like a giant fish bowl with Putin's inflated head somewhat twisted, pushing against the inside fish bowl's glass. The balloon's big woven basket was tethered by long ropes that safely secured it to the earth. Frantically tossing in their backpacks, he got down on his hands and knees, making it easier for his partner to traverse. Like an experienced sea otter, she slithered over the basket's edge. Mel, faster than a fully licensed Hot Air Balloon aviator, prepared for their lift-off. There were four ropes tied to heavy metal stakes. Mel untied the first rope and then tied it securely around his waist. He quickly disconnected the other three heavy cords, tethering the hot air balloon basket to the ground. Mission accomplished, Mel jumped aboard. He could see men approaching, close to where they were. Taking out his sharp pocketknife, he cut loose four corner sandbags. At the same time, a gust of sudden wind had them off the ground just about five or six feet, a dangerously deathly height to be flying. Mel cut two more sandbag weights, desperately pulling on the lever to engage the burner's gas burner. They could feel the brush and small trees making noises, scaping on the bottom of the basket.

Their prayers to get the craft skyward were answered as another sudden wind burst helped alleviate the balloon to a seemingly perfect height and speed as they watched the lights from Putin's Big Top flop disappear from view.

No Loitering or Deep-fried tattor-tots!

Who could construct all the infinite possibilities that one might experience in an individual's life? Like traveling abroad sitting crouched inside a hot air basket being kept aloft by Putin's head filled with a bunch of hot air. Up where time can seem to stand still, floating amongst those lower-hanging cumulus clouds while drifting over the scenic rugged landscape. Both passengers agreeing if they tried to land here and now, it would more than likely result in their demise. If forced to put down the basket in this vast unforgiving hostel wilderness that was below them, they could never survive the desolate conditions they would be subjected to.

Mel feeling secure enough to temporarily feel safe enough to relax, as their air-carriage got pushed west by the steady prevailing winds. "Here ya go darling." Digging through his backpack pulling out a couple bottles of water handing one to Bonnie.

In return, she handed him one of her five-finger discounts from her "food tent" top picks—a sour dough-bread sandwich with dill pickles, sour kraut, crispy bacon, dripping with sauteed-onion-mustard tartar sauce. The two so far very lucky kids were feeling pretty darn happy to be somewhere far away from anything Russian, feeling safer one hundred feet in the air, hanging from a Putin-faced hot air balloon, in a small wicker basket.

Mel quietly praying, "Here's to our extremely long, happy, healthy lives! Which is my way of asking you dear heavenly father to safely get me, and my prison escaping girlfriend #97530 back on the ground unscathed dear lord. Amen."

"Yes, my prayers as well Boss. A very, very long, extremely happy, healthy life! But just in case I wish we had a minister in this basket with us, because we would already be husband and wife and somewhere else other than here, on a wonderful honeymoon. But since there is no minister, were not getting married, this is more than enough to keep me praying that all those honeymoon fantasies one day will come true for me and my guy. Now before we try to survive a crash landing let's eat boss."

Mel divided the Russian circus sandwich the best he could, handing his partner half of the split cabbage-filled sandwich that tasted much better than it looked after Mel man-handled it and mangled it in half. Neither one much noticed as they dined in the moonlit sky. They had been in the air for hours, having traveled hundreds of miles, still heading due west, likely still flying in Soviet air space.

Back somewhere in the Soviet Union Russian fighter pilots were beginning to scramble as they were made aware that two prison escapee's had hi-jacked a hot air balloon that belonged to Putin's traveling Big Top Circus, moving by all accounts west towards Poland by the north-blowing warmer winds.

We're Not In Kansas Anymore
or Soviet Drones Portside!

S oviet Radar and weather satellites had tracked the renegade rouge hot air balloon. Russians had soon deployed fighter planes to the location coordinates carrying programmed drones, that if needed would be employed to shoot down the low flying balloon.

Having finished eating the sandwich they had split. Mel and Bonnie had dossed off and had been asleep when they were startled awake by the sounds of unidentified aircrafts above the hot air balloon's low cruising altitude. They were flying just above the passing treetops, when out of the blue they were being chased in hot pursuit by two Soviet Drones following a short distance behind.

Mel caught in a sudden sink or swim situation, he had no time to calculated what options or actions he should take to defend them from the drones attacks. this modern day flying machine was indeed equipped with cameras. "Quick put this on," handing Bonnie a Putin mask, pulling it over her face. Mel pulled a Putin mask over his face as well to protect their identities. "We need to find some counter offensive weapons, anything we have at our disposal, both digging through their backpacks. Bonnie had found what she considered to be her arsenal of found weapons, which included two baseball size apples, one full bottle of Russian propaganda juice, a lighter, a small butcher knife, some string, and a wad of half-chewed bubble gum wrapped in tin foil. She waited ready, hoping she had everything she might need to fend off at least one of the Russian Drones equipped with cameras, telecommunications, small Projectile missiles capable of ruining what had once been so far a five-star hot air balloon experience.

Tightly holding a hard red apple in her hand, she was ready, as she waited to see what projectile-type weapons Mel had found.

Pulling his hand from his bag, he clutched a loaded gun.

"O.M.G.!" in complete awe. It looked like a six shooter handgun used in old cowboy western movies. "Where did you find that Mel?"

"I found it wrapped in a bar towel stashed behind the cash register in the food tent." The drones were suddenly much closer. There was no more time to hesitate, the two Soviet drones were closing the gap between them and the low flying basket they were prepared to go to battle in. The Soviet sputnics on the balloons tail, close enough to hear the drones simultaneously uttering a message in Russian and then in English: "То Сдавайтесь, или мы снесем вас с неба! *stop immediately or be shot down." Sdavaytes', ili my snesem vas s neba! Stop, stop*

In her heightened alert, Bonnie kept her eye on one drone approaching close enough that this gal who had been the winning pitcher three consecutive years for Ainsworth High School, the "*mighty-mighty-Badgers.* Tightly holding one of her hard apples, she wound up as any tremendously former high school pitcher would—and delivered her underhand fastball.

Mel was just as busy dealing with the second drone's maneuvers, knowing he had six bullets, none to waste. He aimed and shot, then pulled the trigger a second time.

Bonnie had succeeded in breaking the camera off her drone, and it was barely still connected, hanging with one little wire missing its lens.

As if at a country fair, she could hear being asked to "*step right up*," that is what she did, winding up firing off her second apple.

"Thank God from whom all blessings flow," She accomplished her goal when her second apple was a direct hit. She took a moment to view her target, disabled, smoking, spiraling towards the earth. Bonnie, listening to the drome, that was still ordering them to give up, to surrender, falling out of sight into the dense vegetation below.

Mel had also put the second drone out of commission by firing only two of his six bullets. Unfortunately, not before his drone had fired a single projectile, hitting the hot air balloon in the middle of Putin's forehead, before it too mal-functioned and proceeded to drop out of the sky.

Instinctually, they both sat down and hugged their knees, frozen and unprepared for anything resembling a life-threatening crash landing.

"Just like a man," Bonnie proclaimed out loud as Putin's hot air balloon lost its ability to stay erect. When all was said and done, this hand-crafted one-of-a-kind Putin hot air balloon with its wicker-ratan basket would never fly again, although its cargo would live to see another day.

CZES'C' Witaj! or I Don't Speak Polish!

What goes up must come down is of sound logic. That happened as the limp dictator's deflated balloon got hooked on a tall tree. The basket's weight, plus Mel, Bonnie, and their stowed cargo, had bent the top of the tree so much that the basket was sitting on the ground. For a short, brief second, there was no time to see what would happen next. Like being sucker punched in the side of the head, the tide had turned. The tree, combined with the deflated elasticity of the balloon, followed by the wicker basket, had become one enormous slingshot with two kids from Nebraska held tightly inside its clutch! The slingshot strained, pulled back, stretched to its limit. The catapulting took three Nano seconds from start to finish. The entire thing looked like something you might watch on a Universe's Stupidest Videos Caught on Camera television show.

Most of the hot air balloon with Putin's deflated face was flung, torn, scattered into unidentifiable pieces. Humpty-dumpty, had a great fall, and he could not be put back to gather again, the same would be true of Putin's hot air balloon.

"Mel! Mel, are we dead," taking her hands away from covering both her eyes." Mel had hit his head on the ground and was half-stupid, gaining consciousness.

One's destiny is always right here, right now. They were both sitting on the bottom of the basket, which was no longer attached to its four woven wicker sides that had been catapulted up, up and away, disappearing out of view into the sunset. All that was left was just scattered remnants that would tell no tales of what happened to those two people who had been filmed by the attacking drones, both wearing Putin-look-alike rubber masks, from the exact location as was the now undeniable hijacked circus balloon, with its remains haphazardly strewn into the desolate inhospitable Polish landscape.

For now, the task was to organize their thinking, to find what they would need to survive. Both gathered their backpacks, stuffing anything they could use, like the wad of bubble gum wrapped in tin foil. Bonnie put it in her backpack with the other stuff she was lugging around. Like her unopened bottle of Russian Propaganda Juice, a Bicsanova cheap pocket lighter, a spool of heavy thread, and an aerosol can of hair spray with a wide-toothed comb secured to the can by two rubber bands holding the two components together. Plus a few more of the items she guiltlessly stuck in her bag from the seemly endless supply that was free for the taking from Putin's circus clowns makeup crate. How could a clown be herself without a comb or hairspray, and this girl-clown's best friend, besides Mel Porter Dread, was some makeup.

RIP-Torn-Salty-Taste or Gdanske What A Experience!

I t had been hours and miles from where Russian Drones had shot them down, ending their hot air balloon ride. It only took a few moments for the two former circus clowns to pull themself back into reality after their dry splash-down landing ended with no deaths or injuries. Mel knew if they were on Russian soil, they must move A.S.A.P. before a brigade of bloodhounds would soon be nipping at their heels.

"Haste makes waste." Bonnie, shaking her head in agreement, spouted. " Lead on Columbus." How did she know that Mel was looking for a way back to America?

Like any world-traveling sea captain, he needed a ship, or at best, a seaworthy vessel, raft, or small boat. First, they had to find a large body of water. Mel's destination was to get them safely from Russia through Poland to the Balti Sea, which sits on the country's Southern border. The two small-town kids from Nebraska would soon realize they had traveled far beyond Russian-occupied territory into bordering Poland.

"Hmm! I could swear we must be getting near the sea coast," Inhaling another big analyzing sniff of air.

"What are your senses telling you Missy?"

Raising her head, her nose pointed to the sky, taking a demonstrative long inhale of air and slowly letting it out. "I think, I too, can undoubtedly detect the subtle moist hint of salty-tasting seawater, along with what sounds to be seagulls and other aquatic birds." She was going through the motions of appearing to be tasting the air that she was cupping in her hands, impressed by her enhanced and highly enhanced sensatory abilities.

Which way to go was the next very crucial question. Taking one last moment to embrace each other in a loving hug and kiss. Wrapped in on another's arms they whispered one to the other, "Our souls entwined in our minds, hearts, our souls, with God almighty as our faith, guide and mentor," "Amen." "Amen."

It had been a long two-day journey from leaving the balloon's rip-torn and shredded remnants far behind.

"Gdansk," Pointing his finger toward a giant roadside billboard, making their way through what seemed like hundreds of acres of healthy green-topped beets.

They could not see a road yet, just the top of the *"Welcome to our beautiful seaside city of Gdansk Poland." Advertisement on a lighted billboard.*

They had stopped and sat under a group of trees, surrounded and protected by tall brush vegetation. Both agreed it would be an excellent place to rest for the night and regroup for tomorrow. It would reintroduce them to humanity's real-life Circus, where they could go unnoticed in this Polish city of over two hundred thousand or more people who inhabited this city full of rich historical heritage.

Both expert survivalists, they managed to make a small fire, starting by using Bonnie's hairspray and lighter. They both had surprises hidden away, still in their backpacks, so along with Bonnie's bottle of Russian Propaganda Juice, Mel had managed to have selectively hand-picked from Putin's circus food tent an assortment of pre-packaging and sealed snacks Labeled totally in foreign undecipherable Russian lettering, that would not stop them from consuming whatever these Soviet snacks were. By two very hungry pretending to be, starving Russian immigrants seeking temporary asylum in Poland. At least that was their story until they found something more believable than two young Russians who did not speak of all things Russian.

The day would end with Mel's sharing his knowledge of everything history. During World War II, he explained to Bonnie, lying next to him, the Germans invaded Poland to overthrow the country. Determined to make it part of Germany's occupied territory. The world fought back, and Polland pushed the Germans back to where the Nazis had come from. The Nazi's had lost hope of world domination because of Adolf Hitler's devastating defeat. That would end his deadly diabolical assaults against humanity and his commitment to rule the world. World War II, by 1945 had ended. That was the last thing Mel said to Bonnie, who was already fast asleep and did not hear that World War II had ended.

Meanwhile back in Nebraska:

Meanwhile back in Nebraska. Mel's father and mother had good days, along with all the bad days, it was like wishing in one hand, sha-poop in the other. Not a day would pass that his mother and father's conversations, emotions woven with the threads of despair. Hours of worry, all those yet unanswered prayers so far had spun together a heart breaking, disparaging tapestry, full of holes then hung in a place, that no matter which way you look, there it is. Over time that sadly woven tapestry, becomes the fabric we have fashioned into the trench coat, that we can never take off.

The old Dread homestead looked much different than it did when Mel and Bonnie had last been there. The old decaying house and the old barn were no longer there. Both had been demolished, and it was where Mel's parents had a new home built. Its unique design and floor plans were constructed following their son's personal, one-of-a-kind, detailed architectural renderings he diligently loved to work at. Now it had become a reality, patiently waiting for Mel's return, one day, someday, God willing. The rock well where the bodily remains of Darrel, the pot smoking, gold nabbing, stabbing his supposed friends in the back. He was long gone dead, with Darrel's remains buried at the bottom of the family farm's old well. Only Mel and his sidekick Bonnie knew he was buried there. The collapsed well had now been filled in, leveled, and landscaped. An oversized granite bolder sat inscribed with Mel and Bonnies names, followed by a few loving words that ended with, "You are missed, you are loved. In God, we trust."

Next to the rock stood a shiny white cross that Someone had hung two strings of rosary beads along with a dried-out once beautiful Hawaiian lai.

Moving On Up! or Vare Are Chu Vanting Ta Goo?

I t was a peaceful night turning into a hopefully great day to make it into the populated Polish city to find a place to stay. Feeling well-rested, youthful, resilient, and somewhat rejuvenated, having had gotten some restful sleep.

"OK! Mister Hotshot-I got big plans-man. Could you explain how, unlike {The Jeffersons}, we will not be moving on up to a lovely apartment in the sky without money, dough, cash, moola, show me the money."

Not saying a word, Mel began to imitate a magician who was about to pull a rabbit out of a hat. He waved his imaginary magic wand, but nothing seemed to happen, "Something went wrong," as he again waved more intensely. This time around, he yelled, cha-ching, cha-ching, cha-ching.

Bonnie was not impressed one little eye Oda with Mel's joking around about money, giving him her infamous smirk of Ha ha, I do not find this to be funny.

Her acid-laced gaze did not stop Mel's performance, who reached into his make-believe magic black hat/backpack and pulled out a wad of what appeared to be a small bundle Russian currency.

Her mouth dropped open, totally dumbstruck, She could only mumble four words, "Nice trick, hot wheels."

Mel liked the sound of Hot Wheels and contemplated changing his business cards to read *"Hot Wheels Detective Agency."* He would give that more thought, when he could have some new business cards printed-up.

This morning, they were awoken by roosters crowing a short stone's throw away. It did not take them long to get ready for departure. The two kids packed up their things and once again they were on the move, heading towards what appeared to be a busy highway. It was a short walk over the hill between them and where they would hopefully find a ride into the center of Gdansk. They were on a mission to find an inconspicuous place close to the city's busy seaport on the Baltic Ocean. To take time to finally, enjoy time together, have fun, and celebrate being in love. Without any drama, kick back and spend some of the Russian money Mel found hidden behind the cash register in the deserted food tent, which had been left unattended. That's where Mel had found a gun and a bundle of foreign cash wrapped in a towel, then hidden out of sight from the public's good-for-nothing kleptomaniac thieving hands.

"Mr. Hotshot, hot Wheels," as Mel now preferred to think of himself, felt he was simply a chosen instrument of God's intentions. After all, he had always lived his life entrenched in his firm belief that it was "God From Whom All Blessings flowed." That included the loaded gun and the pocket full of cash. It was a gift and a blessing, thanks to his belief in the powers of his creator.

They were standing near a pull-off area, hoping to get lucky and catch a ride that would take them to what was called Poland's Historic Old Town. It seemed uncanny that everyone with a car was in this mod to play taxi cab driver. So many drivers seemed prepared to transport anyone needing a ride for a fee. Mel and Bonnie were looking for the same thing; a room with hot water, and clean beds. Spending little time, they climbed into the back seat of a well-kept 1973 Polski Fiat. " Hello!"

"witaj Piękny dzień dzisiaj, **hallo**, vare are chu vanting ta goo?"

"Old Town, sir. We are in search of a nice place to stay."

"Okies doksie, no problemo," as he wasted no time pulling into the busy roadway driving towards the big city of Gdansk—a world's traveler's destinations. The wealthy young an old, tourist, partiers from near and far came here on holidays, soaking in the sights and festive nighttime activities that Historic Old Town was famous for.

It was a big, hustling major metropolis full of cars, traffic lights, and crosswalks; it was a sea of people wherever you looked.

Their driver had not said a word as he drove down a dark one-way alley, stopping beside a rear back door. Mel held up two paper bills. The driver took them both. He handed Mel a card and pointed a finger toward the building's rear entrance. " Danka, enjoy your stay," and drove away.

"Alrighty now!" Pushing open the Door, Mel slowly entered what looked like a hotel/restaurant back entrance. They could see a young gentleman standing behind a desk some distance away.

Holding onto Mel's hand, "Yea!" Excited as if they had just hit the jackpot on one of those Vegas slot machines. Nodding at the man behind the desk, they smiled. The man behind the counter smiled back as Mel handed the gentleman the card he had been given by their driver. Handing it to a man whose name tag read *Horashio,* followed by five gold stars pinned to his bright blue, yellow pin-striped suit. With a big happy mile, he took a brief second to examine the card he had been handed. "Ah yes, you have been fortunate to be given the Goose that laid the golden egg card. Welcome To our fine establishment located here in Historic Old Town."

"Excuse Me, sir. I know very little about the Goose to which you refer. We have come here as we need a place to stay while visiting this one of many historic cities in Poland."

"No problem. How many nights do you plan to stay with us?"

"For now, a nice room for two weeks. I want to pay cash in advance, and I will keep you informed if we decide to extend our stay."

"Dat vill not ve any problem as vell. Vill yu be paying in American mooney?"

"No." Mel showed the desk clerk some of his Russian cash as the guy tabulated the number of rubles that would be. Mel laid some paper bills on the counter and waited for the man behind the desk to tell him if he needed more or less than Mel had given the guy. It seemed all was kosher as they were handed a room key, several {what to do tourist brochures}, and a paid-in-full room receipt.

He pointed his finger toward the Elevators, "Right that way, Fifth-floor room # 578. Enjoy your stay. If you need anything, please let us know.

Pulling a couple more bills out of his pocket, he asked the man, "Would this be enough to get some food and sodas sent up to our room in about an hour, after we get settled in?"

"Ya vo, vee are known for ore famous in-house kitchen, bar, the gentleman was doing his best letting them know about accommodations here in Old Town. Room service is available twenty-four-seven. The hotel also offers in the mornings a selection of coffees, teas, and an array of deliciously fresh baked goods to help our patrons start their day most pleasantly. It is served daily at Five thirty every morning until ten or so."

'Thank you for that! We both so much appreciate your kindness. Enjoy your day kind sir." Bonnie was exhausted; entering the room, she went straight for the shower. Turning on the water,

she was standing there looking at Mel. " Well, hotshot, why are you just standing there?"

More quickly than a scorpion sting, Mel was now naked. Bonnie reaching for his hand, with undying, unwavering devotion. It took no further persuasion as he followed her into the warm, misty, cleansing cascade of rejuvenating water.

They were toweled and dry after their hour of their joyful reunion with good old soap and hot water. Both were smiling, sitting on the edge of their freshly laundered bed, holding hands, as loud rumbling noises came from their stomachs, reminding them how hungry they were. Mel heard Someone yell outside their Door.

"Room service!" as the echoing sounds of knock, knock, knock, on the oversized metal door. Opening the Door, Mel was greeted by a dapper-dressed man wearing a big white puffy Cheffs hat, matching his Polish black and white checkered servers' uniform and he was pushing a food cart.

"Greetings, please come in. We are anxious to try some of this country's outstanding Polish cuisine.

"Greetings to you as well. I hope you are happy with the Food; please enjoy your meal." Mel handed the man a Russian paper bill, which he politely accepted, then bowed out of their hotel room, pulling the door shut behind him.

They had lost weight over the last two years and were noticeably thinner, and were more than anxious, ready to start eating whatever it was that had been brought to them. They both contemplated the smell of Polish sausage as Bonnie opened several large covered dishes. It all looked and smelt seductively delectable. Smiling at each other, Mel Popped open an icy cold Coke, handing it to Bonnie, then did the same for himself as well, " My dear Bonnie, with all my being, I am bound in Mind-Heart-Soul to spend all my God-given days loving you."

"Mel, you are so sweet," Lifting the old-style glass bottles of cokes high in the air, clinking them, slowly taking a drink, followed by a moment of O.M.G.s. Both agreed it tasted so good, it was to die for!

There were brief descriptions on cards of Food that had been prepared for them. With a terrible Polish accent, Bonnie pulled the cart over near the bed and declared it was "Every man and woman for themselves.

Digging into their Polish feast, they were too hungry to stop and to read what they had been served. It was the "Polish food assortment -*Polski. Stuffed cabbage, pork chops, sausages, pierogies, potatoes, sour kraut, two salads, and a plate of fruit-filled pastries with fresh whipped cream.*

It would be hours before they both stirred from their much-needed restful hibernation.

Dressed To Kill or These Boots Were Meant For Walking!

S tanding at the front desk, They rang the bell and waited for a gentleman to make his way over to greet them.

"Hallo."

"Hi there, kind sir. We are most unfortunate, as we were robbed; they took our suitcases, with all our clothes and personal belongings. Is there a second-hand store somewhere in this part of the city?" In a sad foreign voice, the friendly gentleman behind the desk replied, "I am so sorry fur dat.

Pointing towards the elevators, "Take da elevator," pointing his finger in a downward motion, "to da basements lost and found storage room," speaking in his best English, "Please feel free to take whatever you might use, as anything you take veal not ve missed." Please help yourselves."

"Your so kind." Reaching out to high-five the guy, who had no clue what Mel was doing. With his arm and hand extended, he looked like a Nazi soldier saluting the Fuhrer Hitler himself.

Bonnie smiled at the gentleman and Repeated, "Yes, you are so very kind, sir."

Both kindly told the man to have a good day. Walked over, got in the elevator, pushed the "B" button, the Door closed, and their next stop was the basement. A long moment later, the old elevator came to a stop. The door opened, trying to acclimate their eyes, staring into the black darkness, Mel reaching into his only pocket that did not have a hole in the bottom, pulled out a cheap Russian lighter, and with one gentle flick, was all it would take to shed just enough light to find and turn on the basement lighting.

The desk clerk was right about the years of collected stuff that had all conveniently been stored where else but down here in the basement. Down here, out of sight, out of mind. The place looked like a St. Vincents DePaul thrift store trying to get rid of room full of old-looking, older-smelling stuff, that no one apparently wanted.

Dark Bags Around Your Eyes or Nineteen-Forty-Five Again!

They were excited, like two kids in a candy store. First, they each found nice-looking backpacks out of the many, many choices to choose from. It was the same when it came to selecting a bag or suitcase.

"Mel, why would so many people check out of this Hotel, leaving this massive amount of their personal belongings behind?"

"I have been asking myself the same question "as he was intently examining a dark brown bag that appeared old but was in perfect condition. Happy with his choices in travel baggage, Mel wandered over to an organized rack of men's clothing neatly hanging on hangers. Bonnie, moving a little quicker, had already been busy digging through anything her size in men's or woman's clothing, as long as it fit. She made a few rapid changes before closing and zipping shut her newly acquired bright pink-colored travel gear, declaring she was over this part of the program. Flopping down on a big soft pile of winter fleeced lined coats, she would doze off while patiently waiting for Mel to let her know it was time for them to take their blessed finds, get their precious behinds out of there, and move on. On the other hand, Mel was in no hurry to leave an immense treasure trough of other people's belongings that had accumulated here since the Hotel was built in the late 1930s.

Like any knowledge-filled history buff, Mel had found two old interesting books he wanted to read. "The Hidden Secrets of Poland Finally Uncovered," printed in nineteen forty-six and another which appeared loosely bound pages in a worn leather binder held closed by a taut leather cord looped around it with the ends tied tightly in multiple knots. Its contents would have to wait. Noticing Bonnie had woken up from her siesta. He gathered up the suitcase with an identification tag labeled Joachim Von Ribbentrop's on a tag on the leather bag, now stuffed with his newfound clothes and two books he found from the nineteen forties. What inspired Mel to choose these two books can only be attributed to his innate ability to trust that his life choices can be made of God's Blessings. Given his intuitive sixth sense, he was born to solve and find the answers to mysteries other talented detectives had not been able to solve. Both very much satisfied with their finds, returned to their room with their old/new wardrobe. They would now be totting some splendid looking travel bags, packed with what they considered their going-home attire. Although somewhat prematurely, having not devised a workable plan to return to Nebraska. It would remain a big unanswered mystery that Mel knew he needed to solve.

Mel, no sooner back in the hotel room, was already taken interested in the books he had found, Unlike Bonnie, who had dumped her newfound wardrobe in a pile on the floor. Joyfully leaping in the air. "Yeehaw, Wuhu," landing into the oversized soft-down comforter, where she, before very long, could be heard snoring and mumbling in her sleep with a mellow blues vibe to the sound combination she was making in her sleep.

Mel would spend the rest of this day reading and studying both manuscripts. Both were intellectually stimulating to read. He wondered why two pages had been carefully torn from the leather-bound book. Both books were, for the most part, in Deutsche—lots of black-and-white photos. Mel had become quite familiar with his ability to eins Sprachen si Deutsche— two years of it in high school German class along with two years in a Russian prison where many inmates spoke some German. Putting his books aside, he turns to focus on his newly obtained leather bag containing his newly found wardrobe, and began organizing it. It was a well-preserved vintage leather bag. The name tag still attached, had the year 1946 attached to the handle. Bonnie, still sound asleep was fine with Mel, he kept busy doing his thing and at times like this he did not mind Bonnie's lack of participation. So far Today, she has only gotten out of bed twice, both times to use the bathroom, brush her teeth, and drink lots of water all the time, no matter what. Mel was able to accomplish more than he had expected without her having been a distraction.

He was gazing at the now-empty interior of the leather bag, enthralled with the interior's flawless hand-stitched artistry. His eyes returned to some stitching that, when examined closely, was a different style of stitch, and the thread used was of a lighter color. Like any itch you can reach, Mel was all over it like a sinister case of poison ivy. Carefully investigating the back top of the suitcase, he could feel what felt like folded paper hidden behind the interior fabric. It was virtually undetectable to one's eye as Mel pulled out his pocket knife and carefully snipped enough stitching to recover two pages with handwritten directions and maps. Mel's grandfather was a preacher. Never a day went by that he would take time to proclaim all is possible when you have God on your side. Mel quickly grabbed the taut-wrapped leather book, opened it to where the pages were missing, and was blown away trying to comprehend those two pages missing since nineteen forty-seven were no longer missing.

After the last few days of getting caught up on lost sleep and overeating good ole' Polish cuisine, Mel was now engaged in preparing Bonnie to do her best to comprehend what might be their chance to find where Hitler's box cars full of Art, gold, the stolen Russians solid gold Ember room, this new found map may be the greatest Mystery that was ever solved. He sat there in that moment dreaming about one of the greatest mysteries in the world might finally be solved by a young inspiring detective from a little town in Nebraska.

They had spent enough time doing what they had done for the last few days, and were ready to get outside and begin wandering about this incredible historic city of Gdanske, that sat on the Baltic Sea, where one historic rumor tells us, that near the end of world war II, a German ship loaded with a large assortment of precious luted artifacts, including carrying twenty-seven stolen crates of Russia's famous disassembled Golden Room, is believed to have sunk and lies somewhere at the bottom of this vast body of water. Others believe the Germans loaded their looted amounts of vast treasure on Nazi railway cars. The cars were then railed into one of the complex underground mountain tunnels, which was then blasted shut, burying the Amber room-filled crates, along with the speculation that tons or more valuable Art, gold, and silver remained hidden in the miles of Nazi-built underground tunnels, none has been found or recovered, still hidden. Silently waiting for those who have been searching to one day announced to the world that more of Hitlers vast stolen treasures had been found.

A Hunt For Nazi Gold or By Land And By Sea!

"Bonnie Lou Starr not only do I declare you are the only love of my life, but that today is the first day of the rest of our lives. That said, I have decided today is the day we should venture out and do some detective work. Dive into the mysteries of the Nazi invasion of Poland, where train cars filled with Hitler's stolen gold, priceless art treasures, the famous dissembled Ember Room, none of it, to this day has never been found. What do you say, Missy?

"Sure, no problem, boss. You always remind me that I have nothing better to do for the rest of my life except enjoy working side by side with you, hooked closely at the hips, tagging around helping you solve mysteries. But I could not fool anyone, if the truth be told, I am hooked, line and sinker, on your belief, Mel Portor Dread, that there is *Nothing better than a good Mystery!*" That said, Hotshot, why are we still sitting here contemplating all the hours of trouble we could be getting into?

"Well, Missy, it's not like all that time we spent getting in and out of the shower was as much fun as a guy could have, the most exciting time ever, and I have been taking showers all my life. I now have concluded I will never shower without you there to scrub my hard-to-get-at places" ever again." "Is that some backwoods redneck marriage proposal? Believe you me, I have given the subject of marriage lots of serious foreplay, boyfriend. From the moment I set eyes on you crawling out of that well, covered in stinky mosquito-infected mud, you remember sweetheart, that day I saved your life. We've been through so much, Melvin Porter Dread, and today you have finally asked me to marry you. Maybe after we have returned from chasing wild rumors of Nazi German soldiers—all those illusive legends of hiding box cars loaded full with gold bars and artwork worth billions in today's market. Even rumored to contain Russian's priceless Ember Room which was dismantled and rumored to be amongst the train's cargo. All buried deep in a yet-to-be-discovered mountain tunnel.

Thats the time I start singing "I'm getting married in the morning, ding dong the wedding bells are gonna chime, da da da da, so get me to the church on time."

"I know the answer to your so heart felt rendition of that musical number from Pygmalion. Which was a play by Irish playwright George Bernard Shaw, named after the Greek mythological figure." Scratching his head thinking, further telling that the play premiered at the Hofburg Theatre in Vienna on 16 October 1913 and was first presented in German on stage to the public in 1913.

"You're so smart Mel. How do you remember so much stuff, let alone recall so much of it? When we get back home, I think you should consider being a contestant on that brainiac TV show, what is it called?"

"The Price Is Right," "Hollywood Squares", "Kid's Say The Darnest Stuff?"

"No, Mr. Know it all Hotshot, it's a TV show where contestants try to answer difficult questions." "Hmmmm? "Meet the Press, with Chuck Todd? Giggling."

Tunnel of Love or Proceed
At Your Own Risk!

The game plan was only to stow and carry in their backpacks what would be needed to survive for Twenty-four to forty-eight hours minimum. Mel had paid another week in advance for the hotel room, leaving little else to do but try to decipher where the maps he had discovered suggest the train cars loaded with fortune's whereabouts, as the rumors and stories had been repeatedly told for the last one hundred and eighteen years. The amount of Nazis plundered riches is mind-blowing. Train cars full of stolen treasures believed to be hidden inside rail tunnels in the mountains outside Gdasnke.

If the two should need transportation, they would have no trouble finding a place to rent one, maybe two motorbikes. Bike rental places were big business in this Baltic seaside playground—a fun-loving mecca for world travelers coming from every corner of the world.

"Good mornings" were exchanged as Mel and his partner Bonnie passed by a bushy-bearded, bald man behind the Hotel's front desk.

"Guten Tag, Es geht est gute ya." Laughing, I am from Germany, and my first language is Duesch. You two have a nice day!"

It was a beautiful day to enjoy this fair city of Gdanske, warm, lovely clear skies, what a perfect day to stroll through the old streets of Old Town. Take in the sights and explore some shops while walking towards the city's famous historical Sea Port on the Baltic.

Hand in hand the blessed young couple very much in love, were excited to spent the rest of their lives together. Strolling through the Old Town district on their way to the historically scenic sea port. Both were wearing the woven wristbands they had been given to them by the courier driver. The same man who provided them with the discount card they had used to check in on the first day they arrived at their Hotel.

"It seemed strange, but awfully nice to have been given this handmade ethic matching beaded bracelets. The hotel concierge had wished them of a healthy safe return hoping to spare them from any hidden, lurking dangers from those who live off of others rich red blood. Mel could only assume his colorful remark, *"those who lives off of other's rich red blood."* Was certainly a scary reality in this kill or be killed culture.

"Let's just hope we don't get mistaken for those two renegade Caucasian American prisoners who made Clowns out of the slime-ball dim-witted Putin loving Soviet Union. We need to be on guard, we don't want to expose ourselves to anyone who we are."

"Whoever we are supposed to be pretending to be, let's try our best to blend in and not stand out in the hustle and bustle of the city's tourist crowd, Bonnie tugged Mel's arm, "Hey, have you been listening to me? Hotshot?"

"Sure I was! That's a lie. I did not hear a word you said. Did I miss anything important?

"It will wait. Wow! Look at all the boats, boss." as they approached the seaside harbor, with all it's fast paced, hustle and bustle, of all the boats, ships, of every make and model. The entire seaport emersed in that distinctive fishy, salty seaside smell.

"Missy, let it be noted, my fairest of ladies, A chair is not a chair if there's no one sitting there. A house is not a home, just like a ship is not a boat, and a boat is not a ship. Do you understand the distinction between a boat and a ship?"

She was paying no who ha attention to Mel's need to get his cargo ship full of ego before her small yet significant boat.

Strolling along the pier, the couple soon found themselves standing in front of docked ship where there was a man holding a sign advertising it was open to the public, now serving lunch specials all day long. Those joining them on the upper deck for their dining pleasure, would after dinner, they would be treated to a private tour of this once crucial sea ship that had served to fight off the Germans, defending the Polish homeland and Baltic sea port during World War II.

"Sweetheart let's stop, have something to eat here, the sign says one half off, when we show our discount cards."

"I think that is a simply splendid idea Mr. Dread, as I do have a million and one questions about what the two of us are up to. I think you should take some time to talk to me, instead of me continuing to follow you into, who knows what, ending up someplace for two years in a Soviet Prison. Is that how you define the word partners? Partner?"

Taking Bonnie's hand, he said, "I am sorry, my bad; let me give you a better idea over lunch what I am investigating." Leading Bonnie to board the ship, they were greeted by a man dressed in historically correct Polish military uniform.

"Greetings, two for lunch and after eating maybe you would enjoy, our exclusive one of a kind captivating ship's guided tour?"

"Thank you, sir! Yes, please, two for your all-day lunch and guided tour."

"Right this way." Leading them to a table further away from a small group of men eating and drinking.

Handling them menus, asking, "Can I get you two something to drink?"

"Mel, taking a moment to look over the list of drinks, "I would most certainly like two Virgin Destructive Tornados, shaken, not stirred, in a tall glass, poured over ice, hold the limes. Substitute pineapple chunks instead, please."

"Very vell, Mi pleasure. I vill return with you drinks."

It was not very long and the waiter had returned with their drinks. Waiting close by while they took time to look over the menus, Bonnie had narrowed her choices down to the number three or the number five, which sounded the best choice, it was making her mouth water. "Number five! The sourdough wheat, toasted, extra sauce, deli-style meat platter sampler."

Mel: "Make that the same for me," handing back the two menus to their server. "Very vell, relax and enjoy your drinks. I vill bring you're Food as soon as it is ready.

"Pardon me," the waiter returning to their table with a plate of Polish appetizers, followed by a second man bringing them fresh drinks. "Enjoy, no charge, on the house."

"You know Mel, Mr. Hotshot Defective, I am so glad we don't require alcoholic in our drinks to enjoy, you know, the things like, "She had just experienced a brain fart, staring at Mel with a blank expression.

Mel, raising his dry, empty glass, stops, stares hazelly at it, exchanges it for his fresh Tornado, picks off the pineapple, pops it in his mouth, followed by making a savory hmmm! I love pineapple. These drinks are pretty delicious!"

Bonnie listened motionless, bug-eyed, with a completely blank expression, nodding in agreement with Mel's assessment.

"Yummie', I'll toast to Tasty," putting down his empty glass in exchange for a second tall drink, "Missy, here's to all the loving, caring, friendly people in the world. You know I'm here, you here, were both here. Like everyone, we've met in this? Where are we? It does not matter as our friendly waiter gave us these second drinkie-poo's on him, for nada, "Cheers! He raised his free hand to wipe the sweat off of his brow. "It's getting hot in here!"

"Let's take off all our clothes." Bonnie picking the song up, singing where Mel had left off, moving her upper body and arms to the euphoric music, filling her head with visions of "Nelly, singing Hot in Herre! Ah-Huh, Ah-Huh, Hot?" Suddenly, she feeling alarmingly warm, picking up a napkin and wiping her forehead. "We sure could use a cold drink to help cool us down," she said awkwardly, attempting to raise her drink. Both tried to clink their glasses for one more celebratory toast but were dismally unsuccessful.

"Malevin, hey chu," slurring her words, Mel, did not answer, phissses Melvie, can you hear me? Melve-poo, heloh, please listen to me. Ve may haf beane dragged!" The two "know it all Americans" had been completely Blindsided!

Putin's bounty hunters had planned this scenario that was in the process of being played out. The ship, with its all-day lunch special, a total ruse. Their rides, the hotel room, they were all working for the Russian mafia's underground bounty hunter's organization. All part time employees making a good amount of money by being part of this well-organized crime syndication.

Those Russian Torpedoes had just blown a big hole in their two people row boat. Mel unable to comprehend or to speak. Bonnie, slumping forward in her chair, slowly tilting forward, finally collapsing, hitting her head on the table, knocking over her unfinished drink, which rolled off their table, making a loud echoing sound, smashing the glass into sharp shards, broken and scattered on the ship's metal deck.

Those Darn Dread Locks or Whoops, They Did It Again.

I t would be late the next day when the two Nebraska small-town detectives would wake up to find themselves once again behind bars in separate cells.

By then their Hotel room had been cleaned and made ready for the next hotel guest to be dupped. As always all of the stuff in their room by Mel and Bonnie was taken back down to the hotel basement and placed into long term storage. As few guests ever returned to get anything. Due to they were pretty much mostly dead.

"Proszę przekazać, że mamy dwóch Amerykanów dokładnie tam, gdzie ich chcemy. Mężczyźni z kamerami wideo śledzą ich każdy krok. Łowcy nagród dzielili się łupem i wkładali mnóstwo pieniędzy do kieszeni.

The underground network had been informed, and were very much aware that their hard work had once again had corralled, captured, and ready to be swapped back to the Soviets who would now pay them handsomely for a bounty hunting job well done. Always splitting the money between those involved. This time split between the thugs that were responsible for the two American prisoners having being apprehended.

The two recaptured American Prisoners, a female #97530, and a male #97540, would soon start gaining consciousness. Quickly grasping that they had again been corralled and once again they found themselves entangled in Putin's deadly spider web.

Mel should have known the Soviets would have placed an enormously high bounty on each of them. Two young, stupid American citizens, on the run, is just what bounty's hunters love to hunt, chase and get rewarded with plenty of Russian cash, paid for by Vladmir Putin himself, who would be happy to hear the two Americans had been captured.

Bonnie could see Mel passed out on a metal cot in a barred cell across from her iron-clad cell. She had been trying to get him to wake up, but until now, she had not succeeded. "Mel can you hear me? Mel, Mel Porter Dread, Hey, wake up, Hotshot, talk to me."

"Yah, ya, I hear you. Where are we?" Sitting up on the edge of his cot, finally responding to her many failed attempts to arouse him out of his drug-induced coma. "The last thing I remember is you singing that it was getting hot in here."

"The only thing I might add to that Mel, is now what? You be sure to let me know when you figure a way out of this floating prison. That's right, Hotshot! Remember sitting and having drinks on that historical World War II ship, enjoying our cocktails, and waiting for our server to bring us our meals, do you remember?"

"Oh, it's all coming back to me, I remember thinking that old Vladimir Putin himself could have been responsible for making those fowl drinks, we for a short while seemed to be enjoying!"

Well, mister smarty pants, whoever it was responsible for knocking us out by lacing our drinks, are the same creeps that have us once again locked up behind bars, locked up down here in the belly of the beast.

"Bonnie, I am confident, staring at the cell door lock, "I can open these old type styled locks without needing a key, but only when the timing is right for us to scram. Let's hang around a little longer. You know, long enough to uncover who, what, why, and when? Now is a great time to play deaf and dumb, lose our voices and mime when we must communicate during all and any interactions we have with these grossly pathetic communist pigs."

"I think Someone is coming, Phisss-lie down. Pretend to be passed out."

Heavy metal cleats could be heard, and what sounded like a metal door swinging open as the echo of the shoes got closer and stopped.

It was alarmingly silent. The unidentified stranger broke the taut air with a "Gut dai, mi nam es Symen." speaking in his native language „Proszę, pomóż mi dostać się do Ameryki, błagam. Moje życie jest w śmiertelnym niebezpieczeństwie.

Mel trying is best to understand what the man was saying in broken English. Since this guy was the only game in town, they carefully listen to this Russian man pleading for them to, "Pleese hep me git toa America, I bag of ju. Mi liaf is in mortal danger."pese help mee. "Pese I peg of yu tu hep me, und I vill hep ju. Tomorro neht, yu vil tooken bac tu Soviet junion." Symen handing them their mugshots that were on printed on Russia's most wanted fliers. Then posted where Russia's top bounty hunters went, to recieve all their latest information, leaked to them out of the Gremlin by direct lines to their cell phones.

Mel was reading the words printed underneath their mug shots loud enough so Bonnie could hear. "Every word he tried to pronounce was Russian spoken entirely wrong."

"That makes no sense, Duffus!" Having worked in the prison kitchen for two years, she did not speak the language very well but had become pretty darn good at reading and translating, taking the wanted poster from Mel she took her turn at deciphering what Mel had gotten mostly wrong.

"Wanted dead or alive, two American spies who escaped from a Russian prison. Returned dead, a half a king's fortune, returned alive and unharmed, upon delivery, the bounty increased substantially. That's my take on what it is saying, or something close to that, and Oh Boy, don't we look great in those prison photos of us. We look like two pale American hotshots tightly encased in straight jackets!"

"That's because we were two white-faced American prisoners tightly buckled, tied, snapped, and encased in Soviet Straight Jackets.

"Ya, I remember. Hey, I wasn't watching, where did that guy Symen go?"

" I guess we were too busy looking at these wanted dead or alive posters."

"He made so much noise walking in. I bet he removed his shoes and stuck away."

"He could have. Trust me, it won't be long, and he will be back to pull off his plan to get him, along with us somewhere safe, like the safety of an American Embassy. Hopefully with luck we will get to one, eventually with this guy Symen"s help."

Mel, I hope you know how to get to an American Emphacima. I'm so sorry I cannot be of help regarding Geography-related questions. Still, after two years in a Prison bread factory, I can tell you anything you want to know about yeast and watching bread rise. You know what they say, cash in one hand, dough in the other!"

"No one says that, duffus!"

"Thats OK, call me a duffus if ya like. When we finally get married, sooner, not later, it will be Mrs. Mel Duffus. How do Ya like the sounds of that Hotshot?"

"It was time for them to receive some food from their captors. The same Symen fellow handed them each a metal lunch bucket. "Lat tonite you vil b took by smaller vesail to go n trad yu to Putin's soldiers. I haf plane, geht us out savly hoe yu Amercians sa, Nothin ventured Nothin gained!"

"Symen, we will do anything we can, not to be turned over to the Russian bounty hunters. The three of us escape together, Okie Tokie Symen?"

"Jes, ju eats, gehts soom rust, veri much undar darc ov Neight" Pausing! "Not two vurrie ve hav God un urer side."

"Well, I am guessing he will be back to rescue us, I don't have to work at breaking us out of here, that is apparently part of our newest friend Symen's plans. So let's relax and try to eat and enjoy whatever Symen has managed to come up with to entice us to like him more than we might otherwise."

"I am starving." Opening her metal lunch bucket first, she said, "Oh dear lord, Mel, I like what I see!"

"What did you get?" Opening his metal lunch pail, he declared he was happy as well. Two Cheeseburgers, large French fries, and, would you believe, a cold bottle of Colorado Mountain Spring Water. "Boy these bring back old memories of when we gave up all those sugary soft drinks, and started drinking purified water. Yup! Thats when we both got hooked on Good Old Colorado Mountain Spring Waters."

Stuffing herself, she was moaning about how she had missed good old American Food. "Hmmmmm, so unbelievably satisfying." Washing her Food down with a big drink of her once beloved Mountain Spring water.

Mel was taking his slow time eating, it was rather like the rites of his last meal. He hoped not; maybe his last meal locked up in this tired, rusty tug boat, rumored to once be a respected ship. Bonnie was lying on her back on her bunk, softly singing "I Will Always Love You," by Whitney Houston.

"And I ei-ei......., will always love you-who-oooo, will always love you-ooooo..........Will always love you!"

Duck-Tape Face or Here Today-Gone Tomorrow!

The time was just after midnight when two prominently big men wearing Putin masks barged in, turned on overhead lights, and yelled YU Whooo! vak uppp." Without any conversation, the two muscled, military-looking men unlocked Mel's cell, placed him in handcuffs—and stuck sticky black duct tape across his mug. Finally, putting a black cotton bag entirely over his head. Wrapping duct tape around his neck to ensure the black bag remained covering his face. Bonnie had not said a word, and now it was her turn as the two men opened Bonnie's cell. Like Mel, she did not utter a word while being manhandled, handcuffed, and duct-taped; like Mel, she had a black cotton bag slipped over her head, then duct-taped was wrapped around her neck.

They heard very little conversation as they were escorted to the ship's bow and left the same way, walking down to the seaport main street, the destination, to board a smaller sea vessel waiting for them to arrive a short distance away, Warf-side West to dock 31, Pier 17.

Being led blindfolded was stifling to Mel and Bonnie's senses as they tried not to stumble as they were awkwardly led aboard what was seemingly another boat. Once aboard, the two gaged and bound couple were taken below deck and put in a room with a heavy door that was closed and locked. Alone, quickly focusing like any great escape artist to get the hideous claustrophobic bags off each other's heads. Mel motioned Bonnie to lie flat on the floor like a persistent dog trainer; then he laid down and aligned his hands that were handcuffed behind his back next to Bonnie's head. He feverishly began to loosen and eventually removed the duct tape holding the black bag around her neck. Bonnie quickly rolled and scooted her head down next to Mel's cuffed hands, where he got a hold of the duct tape stuck over her mouth. Like a greased pig getting away, she twisted her head, neck, and body, "O.M.G." was the first thing Bonnie uttered. She now worked to return the favor by positioning her hands close to Mel's head, where she proceeded to remove the bag and get the duct tape from Mel's mouth.

"Shsss! Keep quiet! He was maneuvering to examine the Russian handcuffs they were wearing more closely.

"Malvin, my Mr. Hotshot, I want you to know how much I love."

"Me! I know you do, I love you too, now, please keep quiet while I try to perform right before your pretty blue eyes, mystifying feats more impressive than if done by Houdini himself.

" Professor Houdini, would you mind if I hum? Softly?" "If I can hear you, the answer is NO!"

Humming quietly, Staying Alive by the Bee Gees in a vocal protest. Mel, busy trying to mystify himself, diligently trying to perform a couple more miracles, as now and again you could hear her sing "Stayin alive, Stayin alive, ah, ah ah ah stayin aliveeeeeeeee

"Mel whispering here is some good news, "Missy, who can't stop playing her Squeezebox. I remember those days, when I was always fixated on things, you know, stuff with locks. As a kid, to this very moment, I can honestly say not many locked devices remained locked after I had spent some time working on them, especially older mechanisms like these antiquated Soviet distractions.

Who would have thought that with the belt we all wear daily, with lots of practice which Mel had under his belt? Laughing at that thought, the two, working like teammates playing "Beat The Clock," quickly pulled Mel's Belt off him. Sitting back to back, Mel would attempt to unlock Bonnie's handcuffs simply by feeling and his locksmithing intuition.

You Sure Fooled Me! or
April First Is Fool's Day!

It was a late summer day when Pastor Melvin Porter Dread sat on the front porch with his wife, Angela. Each were sipping on a tall glass of cold lemonade. Having recently moved from Los Angeles, California, back to their hometown of Ainsworth, Nebraska, where they had last seen their son Mel. That was over two years ago.

On this very day, two men driving a black four door Ford stopped in front of the Dread's home. Two men dressed in suits got out and walked up to the Dread porch. "Hello, I am Detective Paul Diamonds; this is my partner, Detective Darin Centurian.

"Is this about our son and his companion, Bonnie Lou Starr?"

Presenting their badges proving their authenticity, that both were from the F.B.I. missing person division, where we were assigned over a year ago. In this case, that we have never stopped looking at potential leads in the hunt for these two missing youths. We have received information from our operatives overseas, who have provided us, {pausing to show them a photo} handing it to Mel's parents to look at. There was no mistaking who these two were, it was a photo of their son Mel and his dear companion Bonnie.

"Detective, when was this picture taken, and do you know where the photo was supposedly taken?"

"Here is what we have pieced together, approximately two years and some months ago. Your two kids had been put on the Soviet Union's most wanted list. Their disappearance was a mystery until we uncovered the photo you have in your hand. The photo was taken from wanted Posters of

Russian news alerts, and it was a constant conversation all over Russia about the two escaped American prisoners, along with their growing reputation for out-foxing repeatedly Putin's plans of ruling the world.

"Detective Diamond, if we don't know their location, has there been any news or leads of where they might be?"

"Oh praise God almighty, we now have hope Angela dear, that they are somehow still alive." "Mam, Pastor Dread, sir, we don't know where they are. We hope to find them alive and well."

Another Russian news story we were informed about, reports that may be connected to the two American prison escapees is that they were also believed to be responsible for an embarrassing Russian circus calamity. Two young adult kids were captured on a Russian circus security camera stealing a substantial amount of cash from a circus food tent. Unscathed, they somehow managed to flee from the mass hysteria and chaos by stealing the circus's hot air balloon, got the damn thing in the air with all attempts to stop them failed. The hot air balloon with the two kids in it, reportedly made their successful getaway, due to strong western blowing winds. Pushing the traveling Mel and Bonnie's hot air balloon towards the Russian Poland border."

"If they somehow made it into Poland, would they be out of harm's way, Detective?"

"Until these two young folks are back home, here in the good old U.S.A., they will never be safe. I will not be surprised if every Polish and Soviet bounty hunter has seen the wanted poster that offers a king's ransom in rubles to return the two kids, dead, or alive!" Unfortunately if captured the last place your kids will ever see is a plane ticket back here to Nebraska."

"We must be on our way. We will keep you informed. Here is my card, it has all our contact information. With all good reason, we are hopeful that after two years, we are close to finding these two kids and bringing them home to you where they belong."

"Thank you, Detectives, for bringing us such hopeful news. Giving us some answers to our years of faith that God would somehow keep our son Mel and his dearest friend Bonnie Lou Starr alive, beat the odds, and return home to us back here in Nebraska."

Shaking the two gentlemen's hands goodbye, the men returned to their big, shiny black car, got in, and slowly drove away. Pastor Dread lifted his wife's hand, gently pressing his lips to hers, and began praying.

Ship, Ship. Hurray! or Cracks In Our Glass Bottom Boat?

The question the two were left to ponder was, ok, now what. They were sure it was only a matter of time before it would be discovered that the two American prisoners had accomplished an impressive amount of resourcefulness, their skill to have been able to removed their head bags, the duct tape that once covered their mouths, but had also managed to unlock their handcuffs and free their arms from behind their backs.

"Missy, take this duct tape, straighten it out, and gently adhere it to the back of the metal door."

Picking up the two unlocked pairs of handcuffs, Mel hung one of them on a coat hook above where Bonnie was now in the process of sticking perfectly re-useable strips of the still sticky-black tape. Hiding the second pair of handcuffs underneath the far corner of the bed pad they had been sitting on.

"OK, Boss! Just know I've got your back to follow your crazy cute ass where ever it takes us, as long as it gets us both out of this dire situation alive." Just another untypical-typical damn dire situation! It would seem we are both extremely prone to always finding someone who wants to kill us! Detective."

"Let's do our best to get into a zen zone. Nothing to do but patiently wait, being prepared to fight when we are confronted by life threatening enemies. Until then, we can only pray that God will watch over us, while we continue to have faith he has plans for us to live."

"Knowing perfectly well we could face our deaths with us begging God for his mercy. What about that unhappy ending Melvin Mr. Hotshot."

"Only fools who doubt the possibilities of Gods miracles, are doomed to fail Gods words of who so ever believed would not die but have ever lasting life, that's what my soul relies mostly upon Sweetheart."

They both would take turns listening for anyone getting near their locked metal door. The plan was to put the black cotton bags back on over their heads. Re-using the black bags as recycled weapons of war, but this time, they had crafted inconspicuous little eye holes, which was a real advantage in any attempts to fight off and gain the upper hand their potential attackers.

They each took turns sitting against or lying down to block the metal door temporarily for a few short moments. Just long enough to distract, confuse, and catch the thugs off guard. "Remember, when played well! Trickery is a perfect decoy to blast a few disabling cannonball holes into the other approaching ship when least expecting the attack."

"Let's see if I understand you Mildred, giggling. We are going to channel the spirit energy of Black Beard the pirate's ghost. Pretending to be pirates on a ship dressed to kill, with a black patch over one eye, a hook for a hand and pretend we are missing one leg, replaced with a hand-carved wooden peg leg. Somehow seems it would take a lot less energy if I just kick the slimy thugs in their vagina's!"

"Need I remind you, we are already on a ship, so technically, you only need to channel yourself to be an imaginary-Bonnie these thugs don't have vaginas!"

"After I kung foo crotch kick the creeps in their under-developed genitals a couple of hundred times, there will absolutely nothing left of the old family jewels except memories. About being on who cares what-we're not on, but rather that we are locked up in this tin can like a couple of sardines waiting to be eaten by who knows how many crazy Russian bounty-hunting sardine-eating pigs.

"Shess, listen, did you hear that? Quick Missy, play dead, and play-act what we rehearsed." Neither one took the time to wish the other to break a leg during this never performed death defying heavy metal song, Vak-op, Vac-up, hay chu Vak-up!"

Like clockwork, both pulled the black bags over their heads. Mel slumped on the bed, Bonnie lying just close enough on the floor in front of the metal door, waiting for the sound of a key being put into the lock. As planned, the man trying to push open the metal door, as intended, was meeting resistance; he got it opened just far enough to see one of the two prisoners sprawled out on the floor, blocking the door, and one passed out on the corner of the mattress. He applied more pressure on the door, pushing the lifeless body sufficiently to allow him to get in. The man was surprised and caught off guard, completely distracted by this unexpected hostage's condition. Bending over to check the prisoner's condition, he began shaking her body. While, in a deep foreign voice, repeating, "vak-op, vac-op, hay chu vac-op!"

You should never turn your back on your enemy, and it was something this dumb Russian thug had consciously forgotten.

Mel had removed the solid metal doorknob, which he now held in his hand. He was as prepared as he could be. Striking this man who was wearing one of those stupid Putin face masks. Mel and Bonnie silently wondered if the Putin masks were what was the current popular trend in the Russian thug's choice of thug wear. Hitting the guy as hard as he could in the back of the head, and one more for his partner Bonnie. Working like dancing partners, performing a perfectly choreographed ensemble. Mel's assistant grabbing a strip of black tape from the back of the door, Mel, faster than Speedy Gonzales, stuck the tape over the man's mouth. Bonnie quickly stuck another sticky strip of black duct tape over his eyes. Like a dead Armatilla, they skinned the clothing off the man, having had removed his outer clothing. Put a black bag over his head tapped it secure around his neck. Grabbing a set of hand cuffs, cuffed the guy's arms behind his back. They had finished up just in time for them to reset the trap and catch another Russian rat.

"Quick Missy I can hear another slimy, stinky Russian outside the door."

Like in a well-scripted movie, right on cue, Bonnie pulled the black bag over her head again and sat her butt down next to the Russian thug, who was still unconscious. Mel stood behind the door, waiting to pounce like a cat stalking a rodent. The door slowly creaked open just enough for them to hear. Helow, helow, it's you frend, Symen.

It's such A Pretty Row Boat or Too Small Throw It Back!

Mel, slipping into the overcoat he had removed from the first Russian slimeball to modify his appearance, Symen completed Mel's getaway wardrobe with, who would have guessed, what all the sleaze bag villains were wearing around this part of the world, one of those ugly cheap ass latex Putin masks. Bonnie pulled a Putin mask over her head as well.

Symen was now in front, leading the way to the deck, one flight of stairs up.

After reaching the deck, Symen opened the door to what looked like a storage room/janitor closest, quietly motioning them both in and handed Mel a handgun, "Pease vait fur me an hare."

Mel helped pull the door shut, then went to work to ensure that the door could not be opened by those trying to break in from the outside. Grabbing two brooms, they each unscrewed the handles off. Bonnie held them vertically across the door directly in front of the handle. Mel found a roll of wire on a shelf and lashed the vertical broom handles to the door handle. "OK, Missy, that should stop hostile Russians from pulling this fortified Janitor room's metal door open.

"Handing a crowbar to Bonnie, he held up the handgun Symen had given him. It was fully loaded with six bullets. Ensuring the gun's safety was on, Leading Bonnie to a far corner of the room, both doing their best to get comfortable for how long they did not know. "Now all we can do is kick back, relax, and keep hoping and praying our friend Symen is our wildcard in this life and death game of Russian Roulette." They could hear Symen out on the boats deck frantically yelling at the top of his lungs.

"Comansi Deutsch, American prisoners have escaped, come, come quickly. Two Russian thugs wearing Putin masks came running to Symen, who was yelling, "dat vay, dat Vay," waving his one hand, signaling the two thugs to come his way, and with his other arm pointing them in the direction the prisoner was last seen running away. One man quickly took off running, to search for the escaped American prisoner. The second man followed Symen below deck, where he unlocked the door, exposing a prisoner lying motionless. "Es he Deed?" going over to feel for a pulse.

Like history has always said, trust could get a person killed. Symen wasted no time, pulling the metal door shut, locking a second Russian inside with the other duct-taped face Russian moron. The second man realizing what had just taken place, became enraged, more mad than a swarm of pissed-off hornets, he began ferociously screaming and pounding on the metal door, that was missing its interior doorknob.

With two slimeballs locked in a room below deck. The two American prison escapees remained nervously hiding in the janitor's closet with the door closed, and barricaded from the inside. Symen, wearing a rubber Putin mask, had been waiting on the pier for the thug he had sent on a wild goose chase, looking to recapture a runaway that supposedly had escaped.

A short time later, Symen greeted the returning empty-handed thug still wearing his rubber Putin mask.

"Da gota vay."

Принес Он мир и благодать, Чтоб все могли познать, Как Бог велик и справедлив,Как нас Он возлюбил (x2) Как нас, как нас Он возлюбил.

Both "Russians were ranting and raving, swearing in Russian that they were in big trouble. They knew they would be as good as dead if they were blamed. In somewhat panic, the two got the small ship unhitched from the pier, headed to the ships command post, fired up the boat's engines, then slowly headed out of the marina trying not to make a wake, as they made their way to open waters, moving as quickly as they could move into the dark, cold Baltic Sea.

Finally Out Of The Closet or Holy Crape Our Boats On Fire!

"Ya got to sleep sometime, with luck the two warn out Americans had luckily managed to fall asleep and konk out, pretty much both comatose until the sound of the boat engines, the up and down movement of the ship's bow being pounded by high winds, and the Baltic Sea's rough waters.

"They both sat quietly, contemplating what actions they should take. Symen had told them to stay hidden until he gave them a signal it was safe for them to come out. With their heads against the door trying to listen for any sounds, when unexpectedly they recoiled, jumping back away from the sounds of someone knocking softly on the metal door.

"Hey Yu hu, it's juer frend Symen. Helow, helow."

Licky split, Mel grabbed the broom handles, pulling on them while twisting them from a vertical to a horizontal position, holding tightly to the gun he had been given. Bonnie stood behind Mel with her crowbar. They were ready to stand their ground and fight if it came to kill or be killed.

"Is it safe to come out?" Cracking the door partially open, Mel seeing it was only Symen. Who he could now see and hear, "Es jest mee, Dat, et wus sevf ta cume oout!" Pulling on Mel's arm that it was safe to come out.

"Let's go, Missy, Symen wants us to follow him."

Mel, and Bonnie, two lucky American kids, followed close behind, two young souls who, like cats, seemed to have nine lives.

Now far from land, the small ship bobbed about silently with the engines and lights off, and ankers dropped. At sun-up, they would try to sail towards Copenhagen, Denmark. Their destination to get to Malmo, where they would seek refuge at the American Embassy.

There were a total of six people assumed to be on board. Two men below deck had been surviving on old military food rations stored in their trapped room.

It had been several hours since they had seen the light of day. If destiny plays a part in our living and our dying, these two bounty hunters, locked below deck will soon die where they now find themselves; two Russian bounty hunting thugs who do not know it, do not have long to live.

The three men up top-side took turns keeping watch through the night. Just before dusk, the ship began pulling in its ankers, preparing to set sail using the navigation compass system to guide the ships destination to the friendly waters off the coast of Denmark, some 562 miles from their current position.

It had been a tension-filled night. Mel had learned enough from his two new Russians' conversations to know they were in the firm belief that they all were as good as dead if they couldn't outrun and stay ahead of the Soviet Bounty hunters, who by now would be searching for the missing ship with the two American kids stowed somewhere on board. It was smooth sailing until, about an hour later when they spotted a helicopter approaching in the distance. All engines were shut down. All those on board hid out of the copter's line of vision. The old play dead lie in wait. The chopper hovered above the ship as a ladder was dropped onto the vessel's deck. A man was soon tangling in the air, making his way down to board the boat. The moment he made his way into the ship's navigation room, the unwanted intruder dropped his weapon, put his hands in the air immediately when three Putin mask-wearing seamen with two loaded handguns pointed at the unwelcomed trespasser's head. The helicopter circled as it waited to hear what the comrade had discovered upon boarding the floating sea vessel. But it would not be in this man's cards to live to report to anyone that he had been captured, being held hostage. He, like others, would spend their few last short moments living on borrowed time.

It would not stop the helicopter pilot from hovering about the ship again and dropping its rope ladder intending to send a second thug to board the vessel. No sooner had the ladder hit the deck than Mel and Symen were ready. Like a well-planned trio, they went to work. Mel was a boy scout and knew how to tie secure knots. Grabbing a mooring rope, you might not have seen Mel tie the boat's mooring line to the ladder hanging from the helicopter if you blinked. All while another man was on his way out of the helicopter, traversing mid-way down the rope ladder, Symen with his gun in his hand, aimed, without hesitation, pulled the trigger, completely missing the man who now had decided to change directions scurrying back up the ladder into the safety of the helicopter. The small ships engines, fired up, the ship moving, gaining momentum, like a tugboat doing what tugboats do; it had the aircraft in its tow.

Broad-Over-Board or My Brief Affair With A Life Boat!

I t has been said thousands upon thousands of times, all around the world, that "all is fair in Love and war."

Nothing seems fair when you lose in any scrimmage involving love or war.

We've all heard about the boomerang effect, as anything stretched to its limit will break apart then like a spring recoil. That happened when the ladder suddenly snapped loose from the rope that held it hitched to the moving boat as too much tension severed the connection with the helicopter's ladder—turning it into a destructive weapon of war, as it shot in reverse and got tangled around the helicopter's blades, putting it out of commission. The laws of gravity pulled the aircraft out of the sky, sending it crashing into the ship's bow violently exploding. Which set the entire ship a blaze, calling for the immediate evacuation for those who could get off the burning boat to escape the flames, smoke, and a fiery death. The five Russian deaths had once again proved, no one knows, like destiny herself, what expirational end-date had long ago been printed onto each of us, like fate, we are either dead or alive!

"zmiłuj się Polish." "Jesus have mercy"

So many times throughout life, we all have had the opportunity to learn that successful outcomes mostly come to those sailors who respect and fear the sea, those that are prepared, to always have a lifeboat ready and waiting, with food, drinking water, life jackets, and four sealed survivor's kits.

By God's grace and blessings, the four, Symen, Bonnie, Mel, and the other fleeing Russian seeking asylum, jumped off the burning ship. Wet, cold, in shell shock, watched as their lifeboat they had climbed into, bobbed up and down, drifting further away from the burning boat. It is a rare spectacular event when you have a front-row seat in a floating raft, while watching a burning helicopter hanging off the front end of your burning ship; with all those fond memories that had been made in such a short memorable excursion, in flames going up in smoke. The grand finale came when the fire ignited the ships supply lines running to the fuel tanks, producing a loud, deafening, catastrophic explosion. Soon, they had floated a great distance away from the smoldering crime scene, or how much of it was left to be seen.

Lost-Cold-Seasick-Adrift or Lots Of Body Ash, No DNA!

This incredibly long day now turned night, as Bonnie closely snuggled with her hotshot partner to help keep one another warmer. Symen and the other Russian sat beside one another, talking occasionally in their native language. They all hoped, believed, and expected there would be patrol boats, aircraft, helicopters showing up looking for them sooner rather than later.

After a relatively calm night, the four awake, hopefully praying that their Lifeboat would be found today.

To be found alive, in a floating rubber boat at sea is a most beautiful thing to dream about. After two more days, Mel, Bonnie, and the two Russians were all starting to realize no one must be searching for them.

"Missy, this is what I am now thinking. After our smoldering vessel was discovered, they must have come to the conclusion that the ship, with humans fragmented bones and ash are our remains, dead people, not us the undead floating out here hopelessly lost.

"Detective, Yes, we can both assume and agree you are right. The good news hotshot is people lost at sea have lived months without being rescued!"

Thanks, Missy. I will remind you what you just said a few months from now. If were still out here floating around and not dead! With us trying desperately to survive when we have consumed all our water."

Bonnie not paying Mel much attention, just continued talking. Melvin, are we about out of water to drink? I remember reading a story about of family, two parents with two children, who were lost for weeks at sea. They like us had soon depleted their supply of drinking water. The mother, a health care professional, poking him to make sure he was paying attention to her. "Ya know what that smart nurse knew Melvin? She contained knowledge that most poor souls like us lost at sea would not. Got a guess Mr. Know more than I do?"

"Let me take a guess miss smarty-pants, who knows I do not like being poked." Taking a second to answer her. "I am about as smart as anyone! My guess would be, that no one knows for sure how long the four of us will be able to survive without any drinking water? Am I not correct?"

"Nice try Hotshot, No! Are you ready to hear the rest of this life saving procedural survival technique, that very few people have any knowledge of." Mel nodding for her to finish her family lost at sea tale. "It sounds gross! Sea water enemas! Mel and although I am not good at it, just know I will be standing right here by your side ready to help administer your life or death, loving sea water enemas, cause I know I might need your help as well."

"We will use that most critically helpful lifesaving sea water enema information when push comes to shove. Luckly we still have a day's drinking water left, lets thank God for that."

Digging through her stuff, looking for something to eat, staring off into the foreverness sea scape, "Mel, I did not realize we were floating around on such a big pond of water, it would be great to see land, huh?"

"It will happen maybe tomorrow. Like the song says, "the Sun will come out tomorrow, bet your bottom dollar that tomorrow they'll be sun." Until then the four sea sick sailors would suffer through another cold night, lost and adrift in a pond called the Baltic Sea.

Change That News Station or Just The Facts Detective!

O ur wobbly world goes round and round until that day, you receive a call from the FBI. "Hello, yes this is Mr. Dread speaking. Nice to hear from you detective. Any news?"

The two men would speak for nearly an hour before hanging up, calling Angela, Mel's estranged mother, to come out and join him on the front porch settee.

"Please sit here next to me, Angela." Patting the cushion for her to sit down. "I just finished speaking to the detective we both previously met, who promised to inform us of any news about Mel and his dear friend Bonnie."

"Good news Melvin or bad?"

"I am sorry to have to say, it's not news any parents want to hear," as tears began clouding his eyes, starting to drip down Mel's father's cheeks.

Angela waited. She did not hurry or pry her husband to say a word. She just gently messaged and stroked her husband's arm and hand.

It was a very emotional conversation. Mel's dad, Pastor Dread conveying to Angela what the detective had shared with him. Now sharing with Angela the information that the FBI intelligence agency had been provided security videos from several cameras mounted around the Gdaske Sea port. Showing what appeared to be Mel and his friend Bonnie getting aboard a ship. A ship that was later found adrift on the open waters of the Baltic Sea. A cruise ship came across the remains of a blackened, burnt-toasted skeletal object, of what appeared to be a helicopter adorning the bow of the small vessel. Which must have caused the ship to catch fire. The fire then ignited a significant explosion, creating what no longer resembled a boat. It now had been converted into an oversized floating designer ashtray. Which had been towed back to Gdanske, where Poland's top-notch clime investigators would spend months, maybe years, sifting through the ashes, looking for clues to the questions they had few answers to. At the same time, they would do everything they could to locate, and collect DNA from the several areas where a body had been detected, at least four, maybe more. It is unknown when any results from the crime labs assessments would be opened for review. This international crime investigates can take years and then end up being put into cold storage, having found no significant leads to keep following.

Time was slowly drifting by, as Mr. & Mrs. Melvin Porter Dread sat on their front porch, not saying much about anything; instead, they sang gospel songs, recited quotes from the bible, and swatted a few mosquitos, driving them off the front porch to go inside, where they both got ready for bed, where they would once more try to fall asleep and get some needed rest.

Holly Mother Of Mercy or Stick Your Finger In The Hole!

The four had managed to survive but now were feeling more dead than alive, having spent over a week lost somewhere adrift in the Baltic Sea.

It is the kind of day that can only occur if you happen to be in an inflated life raft that has suddenly started taking on water and soon turned into a bathtub full of cold Baltic Sea water.

All four clung to the life raft, which contained air pockets that kept the air-filled boat partially afloat. As the skies darkened, the sea's growing waves began tossing them all about, all four desperately clinging to what was left of these four people. Who had been so lucky, and skillfully triumphed in surviving all they had so far lived through. Each one of the lost souls praying they would not die out here at sea. Staying alive, waiting with little hope of ever being rescued, as their time here on earth was slipping away, like water though badly cupped-hands.

God might not have been directly responsible for a Danish fishing boat to spot something that looked oddly interesting floating some distant off their port side.

Dead or alive? Was the biggest question being contemplated by the Danish fishermen as they carefully grappled and hoisted the four unconscious survivors aboard their boat. Wrapping them each in a warm blanket, they were taken below deck. The fishing boat captain had already been on the radio notifying the Danish coast guard with their coordinates. Informing them they had found four people who were near death, but were still alive. The Danish port authorities immediately dispatched a medical rescue helicopter, now on route, to retrieve the four people rescued, all needing emergency medical attention.

How many times throughout our lives do we spend wondering about all those things we keep trying to understand, but seldom do? All those days that we so fondly remember, so many we wish we could relive, all over again. The older and wiser a person gets, the more we learn that keeping busy is the cure for many imaginary problems. Like most well-seasoned detectives, Mel and Bonnie had more than enough exciting stories to share, including how two Russian thugs became their vital allies. Mel and Bonnie, believed the two men, were angels, a gift from God. Without these two guys, who against all odds, became partnered with the two Americans so each would gain their freedom. Teaming up, helping each other flee this disobedient country under the Soviet-controlled dictatorship of evil himself, Vladimir Putin.

All the correct protocols would be followed to the letter of the law. The four of them detained, and processed at the American embassy in Denmark. The two Russian men immediately sought asylum. They would never step foot in their homeland ever again. Both men eventually became full-fledged American taxpayers. Together they opened a coffee shop Pub-eatery named *"Russian Waters."* They had one more thing to achieve to complete their American Dream. The two Russian-born men, now American citizens, would choose not to live in their lie any longer. With good old American pride they had come out of their closets, declare their love for one another, they would eventually get married. As the story goes, Symen and the guy we know only as "that other thug," one of several men who we never saw without his Putin mask. For obvious reasons, both men happily changed their names, which have never been disclosed. The Pubs with modern architecture, laced with old-world nostalgia, was why "Russian Waters," caught on quickly, becoming one of America's favorite places to eat and drink. They can be found across the United States, including Alaska and Hawaii. Countless franchises would be taken out to establish "Russian Waters," locations worldwide, including opened in most international airports.

Nothing Left To Sea Here or Eyedrops For Trouble Vision!

I once was told, "that distance does not always make the heart grow fonder." History could never begin to calculate the endless numbers of souls having gone away for many reasons; to search for a better life, serving your country when called to fight a war. In tough times, couples become separated. Those who left feeling loved came home to a heart that did not always grow fonder. Life is a gigantic all-you-can-eat buffet, filled with all its perpetual ins and outs, ups and downs, and days filled with happiness, joy, and sorrow. Today was one of those joyous days when God answered the prayers so many people have prayed for. The day Melvin Porter Dread III, and Bonnie Lou Star, would return to their beloved Ainsworth, Nebraska, home. A place that hadn't changed much since they had last been there. Except for one brand new premeditated achievement, the decision to build the house Mel had designed and one day dreamed of building. Now completed, Mel's dream home, with its unique design, had remained uninhabited. It would remain un-lived-in, empty until it was known one way or another, until Mel came back to them dead or alive.

That is what Mel's father, Pastor Dread, would, in his hopes and prayers, cling to, along with his cherished holy bible—not a day had gone by that in his daily prayers ask God Almighty to protect, to watch over their two missing loved ones, to one day bring them safely home. The Lord All Mighty was behind the steering wheel, with Melvin Porter Dread III sitting next to Bonnie Lou Starr, in the back seat of a four door shiny black Ford Escalante F.B.I, on their way home. Sipping on their "to die for fountain coke-a-colas!" Quietly sipping, while singing "You are the wind beneath my wings. Lovingly poking each other in the ribs, and giggling like two really happy young kids."

The two returning back home had survived to one day be able to recant to their future children the exciting adventures of detective Melvin Porter Dread III, his partner Bonnie Lou Starr. To one day be blessed with identical Triplets. Mel Dread was a wealthy man who was able to afford anything he needed for his family—blessed by having found those rare 1855 gold coins, each worth a small fortune. In his days as a husband, father, and part-time non-denominal spiritual world speaker. Who would one day be remembered for his continuous contribution to the power of faith and spirituality. His many published books include "Messages From God, "Mind-Heart-Soul-Connection," and his numerous other books that are years later still in demand, on the best sellers list, loved, and cherished by his readers, fans, and followers.

It was the day Mel's dad and mom began waiting and watching for a big, black, shiny, four-door Ford Escalante to pull into their driveway. The FBI agents escorting the two missing kids' home were the same well-dressed gentlemen they had already met and who had kept pastor Dread informed about their investigation as best he could.

It would be late afternoon when Mel's dad and mom stood on the porch waiting to catch a first glance at the miracle that was taking place right now. Not two years ago, not two years from tomorrow, but now. With open, outstretched arms, followed by intense, emotionally filled hugs, it would be the first time Mel had allowed himself to be loved by his mom, his dad. Giving his self permission to love them both back. After a lifetime of feeling disconnected, what a great feeling to finally feel loved, missed, and wanted by the two people in his world he had consciously chosen to accept that was the cards God had dealt him, like it or not.

The young couple had plenty of things to do. Like move into their new house, which couldn't be any more perfect.

Another year would come and go in the tiny Nebraska town of Ainsworth. The population, give or take, averages about one thousand six hundred and seventy-nine citizens.

A photo of Melvin Porter Dread III and his forever and-a-day soulmate, Bonnie Lou Star, would appear in the Ainsworth local paper. The young couple were busy planning a spring wedding, Life now would be filled with memories of that beautiful day when two souls bonded by love, and commitment, were married by Pastor Dread, in the very church built by the great granddaddy of them all, the man who was initially responsible for hiding one ton of lost 1855 gold coins. Which had become just an old unsolved empty rumor. It was a subject seldom discussed in front of Mel. Fearing he too would become obsessed like many others who caught gold fever, then forever searching—but never finding gold. It was now a new generation of young Dread detectives like Mel to give it another shot at solving this long-time family hunt for rumored treasure. It was in that same paper that in a news worthy story telling of Hitler's train cars full of priceless art and wealth of gold bars. When Mel came across the story he was sure the same guys that had kid-napped them in Gdaske, were also the same men who took the book with the two new missing pages that Mel had discovered. The long lost location of one of the German's best kept mysteries of World War II, finally solved. Mel would always regret not being the one credited for providing what had led to solving this masterful hundred-twenty-year-old mystery. The location, where it was found and who it belongs could take years to legally allow anyone to get anywhere near the German train cars now guarded by armed military Polish soldiers.

Melvin Porter Dread along with his partner and forever sidekick, would live long happy incredible lives. Never forgetting Bonnie's first words spoken to Mel, when she found him stuck at the bottom of an old-stinky-muddy bottomed well.

"Hello, who's down there?" "Mel Dread!"

"Mildred who!? THE END.

Goodness gracious no! This is only the end of Mel Porter Dread and Bonnie Lou Starr's latest "action-filled-third adventure story. "Dead or Alive—Putin On the Ritz!" Rumors are flying around AinsWorth, Nebraska, about reported sightings of flying saucers hoovering around the night skies. Thats where our Hotshot detective Melvin Porter Dread, gets himself, and his Kung foo assistent Bonnie, flying higher then a kite in: "Dreadful Encounters with grey Aliens."

mrjohnkaufmanbooks.com

Umm

Oh oh, lay dee odl lee, oh oh lay dee odl ay

Oh oh, lay dee odl lee o, lay dee odl lee o lay

Lay ee odl, lay ee odl-oo Staying Alive!

About Me And That
Kaufman Thing!

M
y DNA would show that I am a hybrid-human alien from another planet that often feels somewhat out of place! You can believe me when I tell you Flying saucers are real! Because the spacecraft I was in crash-landed on a dairy farm in the thumb of Michigan where I spent too many years un-happy and knee-deep in cow poop!

Many, many years later, I continue doing what I love to do, express myself through the many books that I have written. Reading should be engaging, inspirational, funny, emotional, and maybe a place for our consciousness to take a break, and be pleasantly distracted.

Reading my array of books, each individual different. From exciting fiction mystery series, to my life's work of poetry, along with my joy of storytelling in "The Mind-Heart-Soul Connection," I always strive to make life more enjoyable through the magic of reading a good book. One at a time.

To anyone interested in reading more about my life, read my Gold Star Award-winning book "Messages from God—The Complicated Road to Sainthood!"

Please check out: www.johnkaufmanbooks.com

Heartfelt Acknowledgment

Becoming a successful author requires more than excellent creative writing skills; it requires a skilled publishing company dedicated to authors like myself. I am grateful to have found Blue Ink Media Solutions, a business devoted to my success.

~John Kaufman